Maybe Baby

Carol Thomas

Lisa Blake Series

Stories that inspire emotions!
www.rubyfiction.com

Copyright © 2020 Carol Thomas

Published 2020 by Ruby Fiction
Penrose House, Crawley Drive, Camberley, Surrey GU15 2AB, UK
www.rubyfiction.com

A CIP catalogue record for this book is available
from the British Library

ISBN: 978-1-912550-29-6

Printed and bound in Great Britain by Clays Ltd, Elcograf S.p.A.

*To Max and Rebecca, for always
being there, and for all the fun we had
bringing up our babies together. xx*

Acknowledgements

Kirsti Lelliott, for her continued pet-sitting advice and anecdotes. Though I must point out Kirsti is a much better pet sitter than Lisa Blake and has never had an escapee kitten on her watch.

Dean Puttock, for advice on the work patterns and life of a firefighter working within West Sussex; and paramedic Nicky Nichol, for her continued help.

Rebecca Holden and Kristy Carpenter, for advice on Flick's running journey.

Annabelle and Jez Dovell, for their motorcycling knowledge and for sourcing Dom a very nice ride to France.

Amelia, Madi and Edward Thomas, for lending their words and curious minds to Felicity's children; and Sofia Edney who fabulously loves her Mummy 'as long as a tapeworm'!

To all those who entered my competition on the Apricot Plots Facebook page to name the pair of Burmese kittens in this story, and especially to the winner, Kirsteen López Aragón. I hope you liked meeting Kit and Kaboodle.

To all of the amazing new mums who answered my call for research help and advice via my Facebook page, especially: Gemma W, Gabriella, Sarah, Portia, Tina, Reina, Jemma, Imogen, Capri-Ann, Siân, Bernadette, Lisa E, Jessica E, Jodie, Claire B, Claire H, Kerrie-Anne,

Gemma R, Rosemary, Jessica H, Kirsty-Jayne and Kali. I was overwhelmed by your generous responses and willingness to share your pregnancy experiences. Extra special thanks must also go to Rebecca Daniels who let me not only use her cake and poem idea for revealing the pregnancy in the book but also, with kind permission, her words; and to Samantha Harrison who inspired the manner in which the news is broken to the happy grandparents. I hope your little ones are all doing well and you are now getting lots of sleep.

Huge thanks, as ever to my husband Mason, and our children Kirsti, Amelia, Madi and Edward, for their continued support and encouragement, and for not minding when my head is full of the shenanigans of my characters.

On the technical front, a big thank you must also go to: Kirsti Lelliott and Angela MacAskill for reading early drafts and offering insightful comments; and Sue Moorcroft for being an inspiration during a writing retreat in Umbria (your work ethic is amazing, and offers of cake and wine when word counts were reached certainly helped too).

And finally, a very big thank you to the wonderful team at Choc Lit and Ruby Fiction for all they do and the encouragement and support they offer; with special thanks to my editor for her insight and my cover designer for the fabulous spring inspired design. I am also hugely grateful to the wonderful tasting panel (Dimi E, Jenny M, Jo O, Debbie W, Vanessa W, Carol D, Gill L, Cordy S, Kate D, Emily S, Sophie F & Zoe H) who enjoyed *Maybe Baby* – thank you so much, I really appreciate your kind words! xx

Chapter One

When Lisa had got out of bed just two hours earlier, sent a text to her friend Felicity to say she was up and slipped into her running gear, she had been full of enthusiasm. With her long blonde hair swept into a ponytail and a spring in her step caused by the cushioning of her new trainers, she had truly felt the part – ready for action and willing to take on the elements.

Now as the cold wind whipped off the sea, causing her ears to sting, and her entire body felt as if it had gone from cold shock to sweltering hot in the time it had taken her to run the length of the promenade, she was regretting ever leaving the comfort of her duvet. Getting fit for thirty, as Felicity had called it, was all very well, but with her heart racing, Lisa was beginning to think making it to thirty was looking optimistic!

Almost crying from the relief of reaching the pier, Lisa stopped, put her hands on her hips and bent over gasping for air while Felicity caught up.

'I think … I need … an inhaler.'

Felicity's cheeks blazed red. 'But you don't have asthma,' she breathed.

'I think … I have … now … seriously my lungs … my lungs feel so tight.'

'It's just the cold air.' Felicity sagged against the wall of the lighthouse and took a few moments to steady her breathing. 'We can't actually be so unfit that a run along the prom has defeated us.' She rubbed her thighs. 'My legs feel solid; my muscles have gone into shock or something.'

'Mine too … and these trainers have given me a

blister.' Lisa slipped her foot out of her trainer, revealing a once-white sock now reddened at the heel. 'So much for revolutionary comfort … and bloody "responsivity". I knew that had to be a made-up word.'

Lisa looked from her shoe to Felicity, and they both laughed. As their laughter turned to sighs, they stood for a while, leaning against the lighthouse wall, watching the waves crash against the pier.

Eventually, Felicity spoke. 'Well, we might not have the right gear, and we might be unfit, but at least we've made a start. By the time May comes, and we head to France for our girly weekend, we'll be fabulously fit. You'll see.' Felicity put her arm around Lisa's shoulder as they began to hobble back along the prom, to the car.

'I can't wait.' Lisa smiled focusing on the trip and how wonderful it would be to celebrate her birthday with Felicity.

'Me neither.' Felicity sighed, adjusting her leggings. 'Did I mention my leggings are chafing in places I didn't think possible?'

'No. Did I mention my boobs feel like they've gone three rounds with Anthony Joshua, and not in a good way?' Lisa added.

'Now there's a thought.'

'Behave.' Lisa nudged Felicity in the ribs.

'You started it. Besides, I can't behave. I blame my husband! You'd think whisking me off to see the new year in, in Barbados, would have seen me satisfied for the year, but no. It's reminded me what I've been missing. Since we've been back, I can't get enough of him. It's partly why I want to get fitter, build my stamina.'

Lisa laughed. 'Felicity Willis, you are insatiable.' Spotting the East Beach Café in the distance, she continued, 'And talking of insatiable appetites, I'm hungry. We must have earned a few calories, maybe even enough for a fry—'

Lisa and Felicity fell silent, their mouths open, as two women ran effortlessly past them. They watched as the older, fitter pair pounded their way along the prom in unison. The women's cheeks were barely red, and their running clothes put Lisa and Felicity's make-do efforts to shame.

Felicity's eyes followed them. 'You know, with the right gear and a bit more practice, that could be us.'

So that's a no to the fry-up, then. Lisa sighed as they both turned and continued towards the car. She admired Felicity's optimism, but the way she was feeling, Lisa doubted that daily practice in a Mo Farah boot camp could turn her into a runner. If the morning had confirmed anything in her mind, it was that running was not her thing. Upon reflection, it never had been; she had hated it at school and avoided it as an adult. With her lungs still burning, but the wind making the sweat on her body turn cold, Lisa was finding it hard to remember why she had agreed to go along with it at all.

OK, so she had put on a little weight over the festive period, but wasn't that a generally accepted seasonal hazard? After all, December was the month of excess – the time when consuming crystallised fruit-flavoured jellies or a whole chocolate orange legitimately counted towards your five a day. But the weight gain wasn't something she was concerned about. Lisa was starting the new year confident the pounds would soon drop off: being a pet sitter and dog walker, she had an active job; she was eating fewer Chinese takeaways; and she was getting plenty of exercise courtesy of her rather lovely, attentive boyfriend, Nathan. Just thinking about him made her smile.

Felicity made an 'aww' sound that caused Lisa to look at her.

'I'm so pleased you're smiling. I was worried back there, you might have hated it.'

I definitely hated it.

'But it's good, isn't it? I mean ... not this.' Felicity motioned between herself and Lisa. 'The state we're in now, that's not good, but the fact we're out of the house, taking on a challenge and trying something new.'

And there it was, the reason Lisa had agreed to go on the run. Not because she felt the need to lose weight or get fit for thirty, not because she needed a challenge – she was still building her business and had her new relationship with Nathan to focus on – but because Felicity needed those things. Having not always been there for her, Lisa wanted to offer her support, to step up and be a good friend, the way she had been before her time spent travelling and living with her ex-partner Ben had got in the way. But, while Felicity continued to talk about how great it would be for the two of them to put their names down for a 5K, Lisa realised she needed to work out how she could continue to step up without stepping out in running gear!

The car was a welcome sight. Felicity opened the door and got in while Lisa took her fleece from where she had left it on the back seat and slipped it on. Sitting in the passenger seat, she rubbed her hands together to breathe life into her numb fingers before taking out her phone. Felicity started the engine in readiness to pull away, but paused, raising an eyebrow at Lisa's crestfallen expression.

'What's up?'

'Nothing.' Lisa slipped her seatbelt on. 'Nathan and I were meeting for lunch, but he's letting the flat below him to an old friend for a while—'

'I still can't believe he owns that whole building. Your boyfriend, the property magnate. Whoop, whoop.'

Ignoring Felicity's laughter and nudges, Lisa continued, 'Anyway, they were meant to be arriving next week, but Nathan says *she's* turned up a week early.'

Taking in Lisa's expression, Felicity frowned. 'Is that a problem?'

'No. Of course not. We're going to catch up later.' Lisa attempted a smile, put her phone in her lap and put her seatbelt on. 'It's all sorted.'

Felicity checked her mirrors, indicated and pulled out. 'Are you sure? Only if you can't wait that long to see him, I could drop you there now.'

'Ha, I definitely don't want to meet *her* in this sweaty state—'

'Ah, so it's the fact it's a female friend, that's what the problem is.'

'No. Yes. Well, maybe.' Lisa groaned, wondering why she had automatically assumed it would be a male friend.

'Well, I'm glad that's clear.'

Lisa swiped her hand at Felicity and tried not to glance too obviously towards Nathan's building as they drove past the corner of the road he lived in. 'It's just it seems a bit weird, that's all. Meeting friends is always a part of being with someone new. But Nathan's not new, not really, yet this woman knows him, and I've never met her.'

'Well, that's not surprising when you've only been back together, what ... weeks? A couple of months, maybe, depending on when you're counting from.'

'I know. It's just she's from the time we were apart. Eleven years is a long time. We've gone from secondary school sweethearts where we knew everything about each other to now being boyfriend and girlfriend with unknown pasts. She'll know things about him I don't. They'll have shared experiences. And I don't know if they've always been friend

5

friends or if they've ever been *"friend* friends".' Lisa made air quotes around the final words to express the point.

'Does it matter? You're the person he's recently told he wants to spend the rest of his life with. The person nobody else matched up to in the eleven years you were apart. You don't need to worry about her, not if she is a friend or even if she was ever something more. Nathan's in love with you. He always has been.'

Lisa glanced out of the window, noticing how short the prom seemed when you drove along it. 'I know you're right.' She picked up her phone to reply to Nathan's messages but smiled when she saw a new message from him, with the promise of a leg massage when he saw her later.

As Lisa typed her reply, Felicity glanced at her. 'And you know you could ask him, share what you're thinking. Have a conversation about it. That's what couples do.'

Lisa nodded, but knew she wouldn't share her concerns with Nathan. Jealousy was ugly, and it could be cruel. Her years in London with her ex-boyfriend Ben had taught her that.

'All that matters is what's between you two. If you're both open and honest about your feelings and ... and the time you were apart—'

'Ha, nice segue there, Flick, very smooth.' Lisa folded her arms, the warmth from the car heater doing nothing to dispel her goosebumps. 'And I will tell him. It's just hard to find the right time.'

'What, like ... oh, I don't know, during an evening together? When it's just the two of you? If only the opportunity would arise.'

Lisa rubbed her hand across her wind-battered forehead and thought about the conversation Felicity was referring to, the one she knew she had to have with Nathan but had been putting off.

Chapter Two

Having sent a text to say she was on her way after dropping Lisa off, Felicity got home to find Pete and the children preparing breakfast. Megan was helping Pete with the cooking, Alice was laying the table, Callum was stacking the variety packs of breakfast cereal, and Fred, well, Fred had a saucepan on his head that he was hitting with a wooden spoon – but he thought he was helping. She gave each of them a kiss, removed Fred's saucepan and passed him a tub of less noisy but equally entertaining pastry cutters from the drawer.

'How was the run?' Pete took the bacon out of the fridge.

Felicity slumped into a chair at the table. 'Torture! I am so unfit. I thought I was going to die.'

'What?' Callum stopped stacking the cereal.

'Not really, darling, it's just something people say. It means it was very hard work.' Felicity sat up, attempting to look less exhausted than she felt.

'But people do die from running,' Alice offered as she placed the last set of cutlery on the table.

'Do they?' Callum's eyes went wide.

'No. They don't!' Pete glared at Alice, putting his finger to his lips.

'But they do. You remember on the radio they said—'

'Oh, here we go,' Pete muttered under his breath.

'Alice, that's enough.' Felicity gave her an admonishing glare. 'I jogged along the beach, it was hardly a marathon, and don't you worry, Pumpkin, Mummy is fine.' Felicity went to ruffle Callum's red hair but missed as her son and everything in the room seemed to shift sideways. Feeling light-headed, she swaggered and sat down, holding her head.

Pete grabbed a glass from the cupboard, filled it with water and took it to her.

As Felicity sipped the cool water, the dizziness subsided. She took a slow, steadying breath and looked up, noticing the eyes of all her children upon her. She gave them a reassuring smile. 'Honestly, I'm fine. I just didn't eat before I exercised, I probably didn't drink enough, and—' she lifted her arm and sniffed '—I need a shower. But other than that, I'm good.'

Pete crouched in front of her, meeting her gaze, a silent check she was really all right.

Felicity smiled and nodded, feeling the after-effect of the dizzy spell in the movement.

Pete looked at the children. 'See, Mummy's OK. We'd better get this breakfast finished so she can eat.' He stood, encouraging the children to crack on with their jobs, before glancing at Felicity. 'Why don't you stay there, drink that, and eat before you get cleaned up? The food's almost done.'

'Really, I'm fine.' Felicity stood, holding the edge of the table as she tested her balance. 'I'll have a quick shower while you finish off, and then I'll really be able to appreciate this lovely breakfast.'

'But—'

'I'll be five minutes.' Picking up her water, Felicity headed upstairs – her leg muscles aching from the run and her head feeling foggier than she was willing to admit.

In the bathroom, she turned on the shower and peeled off her clothes. Her thighs were mottled red from the shock of exercise as much as windburn, and she was certain she would be suffering by the following day, but she didn't care. Fred was two; it was time she found herself a hobby, and why not running? Standing under the hot shower, Felicity reasoned that with time, she could be every bit as fit as those women who had run past her and Lisa so effortlessly – in their appropriate running gear and annoyingly composed state. She just needed to set herself reasonable goals broken down into smaller targets. The 5K she had mentioned to Lisa would be achievable if she worked towards it. With that in mind, Felicity thought about her first targets. *Number one: invest in running clothes that won't chafe. Number two: make it the length of the prom without feeling—*

A knock at the door and a shout from Megan to say breakfast was being dished up made Felicity jump.

'Coming.' She reached for her towel and rubbed her feet and legs dry before stepping out of the shower on to the tiled floor.

'Daddy says two minutes.'

'Almost done.'

Drying quickly before wrapping the towel around herself, Felicity went to open the window to let some steam out of the room. But in her haste, she knocked the metal spice rack she used as a bathroom tidy sideways. It crashed to the floor; earbuds, tampons, cotton wool, various bottles of forgotten lotions, baby oil and talcum powder scattered in different directions. 'Bugger—'

'What was that?'

Realising Megan was still by the door, Felicity held back the rest of the expletives she wanted to say.

'Mummy, what happened?'

'I knocked the ...' Felicity paused, searching for a word suitable for her daughter's ears, 'stuff ... off the shelf.'

Crouching to start the clear-up operation, Felicity heard Pete call from the bottom of the stairs.

'What was that?'

'Mummy knocked the stuff off the shelf.'

'You OK, Flick?' Pete's voice came again.

Felicity didn't answer.

'Mummy?'

'Err … I'm … fine.' Felicity knew she should answer with more conviction, her voice sounded shaky, and Megan was a worrier; she needed to reassure her. But sitting crouched, staring at the mess, holding the empty tampon box in her hand and reliving the dizzy feeling she had felt in the kitchen, the words would not come. It was a feeling she knew she had felt before. A feeling she thought she wouldn't have again. Staring at the empty box, its contents scattered amongst the bottles, balls of cotton wool and earbuds on the floor, she wondered when it was she had last used them – when had she last had a period? *Before Barbados.*

Pete's footsteps thudded up the stairs. 'Flick?' He rattled the handle. 'Megan, go and check on the others.'

'But, Dad—'

Before Christmas.

'Go on. I'll help Mummy.'

Before Christmas shopping.

'Flick, open the door.'

How long before then?

'Felicity!'

She heard Pete fiddling with the outside of the lock – she knew he could open the door. He'd done it before when Fred locked himself in and again when Alice had secretly been making potions and was trying to test them on Callum. The realisation dawning on her, Felicity stood up. Pete couldn't find her dumbfounded, crouched on the floor. She couldn't offer an explanation, not one she wanted to be true, or that she was ready to share. She pulled open the door, and her eyes met Pete's. He looked at her and at the mess.

'Are you all right? Why didn't you answer?'

'Sorry. I ... I'm fine—'

'But—'

'I've knocked the stuff off the shelf. That's all.' She started acting on autopilot, picking up the things that had dropped. 'I'll be down in just a minute.'

'I'll help you.'

'For goodness' sake, Pete. It's fine. Everything's fine.' *It has to be fine.* She knew she sounded horrible, that Pete was just checking on her, making sure she was OK – the way he always did. She breathed and attempted to smile. 'I'll do this. You sort the children.'

Pete looked from the mess to Flick and then down the stairs, clearly torn as to what he should do. 'You sure?'

'Yes. They'll burn the bloody kitchen down if you leave them much longer.'

'Everything's in the oven now.'

Felicity looked at him, raising an eyebrow.

'Good point.'

'I'll be down in two minutes.' With that, Felicity shut the door and picked up the rest of the mess. Before leaving the bathroom, she slipped off her towel and looked in the mirror. There were no tell-tale signs. Her breasts looked the same as they always did. She felt and looked her normal self. Flick wrapped the towel back round herself, pulling it in a little tighter. Just because her periods were normally like clockwork, just because she hadn't missed one before without being pregnant didn't mean the stress of Christmas or the shock of going to Barbados couldn't have thrown her cycle out. *Did it?* There had to be a logical explanation. There just had to be, because women whose husbands have had a vasectomy don't just get pregnant. *Do they?*

Chapter Three

After a shower, a coffee and a doze in the armchair in her mum's conservatory, Lisa felt human again. She wasn't sure her legs would forgive her anytime soon, but she was finally warm, and her ears had stopped burning from the chill of the wind. As she had no dogs to walk in her diary, her morning cat visits had been taken care of before her run, and feeding the Burmese kittens, Kit and Kaboodle, would fit in nicely en route to Nathan's, she wondered what to do with herself for the rest of the day.

Lisa fetched her laptop and flicked to her Facebook business page. Keeping it updated was a New Year's resolution she had promised herself she would stick to. Staying in her parents' home was all very well while they were in France, but with them due home for six months from Easter, she knew she had to think about getting a place of her own. Growing her business was integral to making that happen. Building her reputation and client base through recommendations was great but slow, so she had also been thinking about other ways to increase her income. A dog-grooming course at the local college looked appealing. Lisa knew from her days of working on *Paws About Town* magazine people would pay a fortune to have their pooch looking pristine. She needed a plan, she needed to focus and she needed to make it happen.

About to get a piece of paper to make a list of ideas, she noticed a text from her friend, Dom:

'Jack and I miss you. Free for lunch? Jack fancies the pub, but you know Labradors, anywhere with food and a warm fire will do.'

Lisa laughed. Other than a quick call from Dom to let her know he'd recommended her pet-sitting services to a colleague with a feisty rabbit, it had been a couple of weeks since they had caught up properly; lunch sounded perfect. She texted a quick reply to say she would meet them at one. As she went to get ready, an idea occurred to her. She knew Felicity was right; she really did need to be open and honest with Nathan about her past. But the thought that hearing what she had to say might hurt him, or worse make him rethink their future together, scared her. Even contemplating the conversation put her stomach in knots. Maybe Dom could offer her a man's perspective? She could share it with him. He was her friend, just as Felicity was. If she told him, maybe he could help her gauge what Nathan's reaction might be. Speaking to him might give her the courage she needed to face the conversation. And she knew Dom could keep a secret. He was a paramedic after all, not only would he have seen all sorts, but he would have taken some kind of medical oath, like a doctor – *wouldn't he?*

Just before one o'clock, Lisa pulled open the door of the pub to be welcomed by warmth, a hubbub of noise and the mouth-watering smell of Sunday roast. She smiled at the bartender's greeting and glanced at the blackboard – roast lamb, chicken or gammon, and a host of traditional desserts her Granny Blake would have been pleased to serve. Comfort food, just what she needed after the cold start she'd had to the day. Her stomach rumbled.

Lisa glanced beyond the tied-back curtain at the end of the bar, to the dining area. Dom waved from a table adjacent to the open fire, and Jack lurched forward with a bark at the sight of Lisa. His lead unwound from the table leg, and he excitedly dragged it across the well-worn flagstone floor with a clatter as he went to meet her. Lisa crouched to greet him, welcoming his slobbery kisses.

Catching Jack's lead, she headed over to Dom – the excited Labrador bouncing along at her side.

Dom stood and hugged her. 'I'm not sure I can match that welcome.'

'I should think not, you'll get us thrown out, and I'm starving.'

Dom reattached Jack's lead to the table leg before offering to go to the bar for drinks, but the smell of the food was making Lisa's stomach rumble.

'Do you know what you want to eat? If so, I'm ready to order.'

'You don't waste any time, do you?'

'The blackboard had me at gammon.' She laughed, deciding not to mention she had already planned her apple pie and custard dessert too.

After ordering two roasts with all the trimmings, Dom returned to the table carrying a Diet Coke for Lisa and sparkling water for himself.

With Jack's front paws on her knees, Lisa peered round the dog's head. 'I don't know what is with this dog; he won't leave me alone.'

'He's missed you. That and he can't believe he's been stuck with me looking after him for the past couple of months.'

'Hmmm, well, we've always got on, Jack and I, but I'm not sure he's ever loved me quite this much.' Lisa pushed Jack's chest, encouraging him to take his paws off her, as he once again attempted to get on her lap.

Dom called Jack to his side and gave him a stroke. 'Am I that bad that you're trying to get Lisa to take you home?'

Jack tilted his head.

'Ah no, he loves you. Look at those adoring eyes. He probably misses Winnie, that's all; when is your gran home?'

'Next weekend and then normal service can resume. You can be Jack's dog walker once more, and I can invite friends back to my place without the risk of Jack here drooling on them.'

'Friends?' Lisa raised her eyebrows and shifted forwards in her seat.

'Yes, friends. Just friends. Not what you're thinking.'

Lisa sat back. 'Ah, shame. So ...'

'No. No boyfriend. Nobody for you to get excited about.'

Lisa wondered if she could push the subject. Having not long come out to her and his gran, Lisa knew it would take Dom a little time to feel confident discussing his love life. But she hoped for his sake someone special was round the corner. She had only known him since she had started walking Jack, but it was long enough to know he was lovely and not just because he was a hot paramedic who also rode a motorcycle and looked quite something in his leathers. He was sweet, kind and funny. He deserved the type of happiness she had found with Nathan. She wanted him to know he could speak to her about anything and anyone. Just as she hoped she could with him. Lisa swallowed, wondering if now would be a good time to broach the subject of the conversation she needed to have with Nathan. Taking a deep breath, she went to speak but stopped as Jack's head slumped onto her feet. 'Will you look at this silly dog?'

Big eyes looked up at her as the grey-bearded dog did his best to look every bit the innocent puppy, having crawled commando-style across the floor to be near her.

'Maybe it's your perfume.' Dom laughed as their dinners were placed on the table in front of them, and they declined the offer of sauces.

Jack sat up sharply at the smell of the food.

'Well, if it is my perfume, it's obviously not as good as the smell of this roast.' Lisa pulled her plate closer to her and looked at Jack. 'Forget it, mister, this is mine!'

After consuming what felt like an awful lot of food and succumbing to a few fortifying glasses of wine as their conversation had progressed, Lisa stretched and glanced at her watch.

'Oh my goodness, it's half four. How did that happen?'

'It takes a while to eat that much food.' Dom's eyes flicked to the empty dessert bowls on the table.

'That's very polite of you, but I know I've been talking for ages. I'm sorry.'

'No, seriously, I can't remember the last time I ate so much.' Dom rubbed his stomach.

'But—'

He leaned forward and placed his hand on hers to stop her. 'Lisa, it's fine. I'm happy to listen, and if talking to me makes you feel ready to speak to Nathan, then that's a good thing.'

'Thanks, Dom, you're a good friend.' Lisa felt drained. The conversation, the warm fire and her full stomach made her want a sleep rather than have a long-overdue heart-to-heart, but she knew she couldn't keep putting it off.

Lisa took her phone out of her bag and saw a missed call from Felicity as well as three messages from Nathan. Not wanting to commit to another run, she sent Flick a text saying she was sorry to have missed her, she hoped her legs weren't too sore and she'd catch up later. She scrolled to

Nathan's messages – one asking how her run had gone and apologising that he hadn't asked before, another saying he loved her, and the final one saying he'd cook and would have food ready for half five.

'Oh no!'

'What is it?' Dom looked at her.

'Nathan's cooking me dinner.'

Dom laughed. 'Oh, you're buggered. Did you ever see that *Vicar of Dibley* where she eats all those Christmas dinners?'

'It's not funny. What am I going to do? He says it will be ready at half five. I'm stuffed, I've still got Kit and Kaboodle to feed, and I drank all that wine. I can't even drive now. I thought the walk would clear my head ... but—'

Sensing Lisa's panic, Jack started jumping up and panting.

Dom stood and took hold of Jack's collar. 'It's fine. I can drive you. We can feed the kittens on the way. Then I'll drop you at Nathan's, you can tell him you missed his message, you've already eaten, and you can reheat whatever he's cooked tomorrow. Nathan's a reasonable person, Lisa. He's not going to mind.'

Lisa knew Dom was right; Nathan was a reasonable person, unlike Ben. She had to remind herself of that. 'You're so bloody calm and sensible. Please tell me there are some situations where you get completely fazed like the rest of us normal human beings.'

'Being calm is my superpower.' Dom laughed as they thanked the barman on their way out the door.

'Really, and that's all you've got to offer me right now? Nothing better? Nothing cool, like turning back time to before I ordered and ate so much food?'

'Nope, Captain Calm, that's me.' Dom winked.

'Well, right now, Captain Calm, all that's likely to get you is a punch.' Lisa giggled, punching Dom's arm playfully.

Standing in front of the Edwardian house, Lisa rummaged for her key. While, as a firefighter, Nathan worked regular shifts, he had said there were times when he might be detained on a shout and didn't want to leave her stranded. As being stranded at Nathan's and unable to get in would have simply meant she was ten minutes from home, she had protested. But as the intercom frequently played up, and Lisa realised the reason for Nathan's offer of the key was his way of making a sweet gesture while trying not to appear to move too fast too soon, she had accepted.

Lisa walked up the stairs towards Nathan's flat on the top floor. Her legs didn't feel too bad, but she was looking forward to the massage Nathan had promised, *maybe in front of a warm fire, with a glass of wine*. The thought made her smile, as did spotting the man himself leaving the door of the flat below his. She soaked in the sight of him – trainers, jeans and a navy T-shirt that revealed honed muscles. His dark blond hair was ruffled, and he hadn't shaved. *Perfect!* As he turned away from the door to continue up the stairs, she spoke.

'And there I was thinking you were slaving over a hot oven for me.'

Nathan raised his eyebrows, his blue eyes meeting hers and a mischievous grin tugging at his lips. It was a look she liked.

'Well, a broken boiler and landlord duties called, but don't you worry, your food is ready.'

Lisa tried not to think about the still too-full feeling she had from the roast dinner, as Nathan walked down the few stairs between them. She welcomed his kiss and smiled as he motioned for her to lead the way up to his flat.

'I'm never sure if you're being a gentleman or if you're looking at my bum when you let me go first.'

Nathan laughed. 'Is it wrong to say both?'

'I knew it!' Lisa giggled and started running up the stairs, regretting the sudden effort almost instantly.

Nathan grabbed at her, and she squealed, dismissing the ache in her legs as she ran faster until she reached the flat door. It was ajar, so she ran straight in, laughing, but as her eyes met the sight before her, she stopped. 'That's not—'

Nathan burst through the door behind her. Halting and letting out a breath as he took in the scene.

'—what you expect to see when you enter your boyfriend's flat,' finished the woman, who was wearing an all-over tan and a too-small towel. She padded across the floor towards them with her hand out.

Lisa realised she should probably close her mouth, say something, ask the many questions flitting through her head, but all she could do was stare, eyes wide, between Nathan and the woman before her. Her heart was thudding, causing blood to rush in her ears, and she was pretty sure it wasn't due to the run up the stairs.

'I'm Sam,' the woman said, her smile revealing straight white teeth. Her chestnut-brown hair was pulled into a messy bun, and her bare shoulders glistened, still wet from the shower.

'Bloody hell, Sam, when I said have a shower, I didn't expect …' Nathan pushed his hand through his hair, before continuing, 'Lisa, this is Sam.'

'I've said that.' The woman laughed, dismissing the disapproving tone in Nathan's voice as she shook Lisa's hand.

Lisa looked at Nathan, removing herself from Sam's manicured grasp.

The woman grinned. 'I'm a close friend of Nate's.'

'Staying in the flat downstairs.' Nathan added, or corrected – Lisa wasn't sure which it was. 'Her boiler wasn't working. So I said she could use the shower up here. I didn't think …' His words trailed off.

Sam lifted her shoulders into a shrug as she smiled innocently. The action caused the towel to strain at her bust and rise further up her thighs.

Lisa bit her lip, unsure what would come out of her mouth if she spoke.

'Anyway, you're done now, right? So you should get some clothes on. The boiler's fixed, and Lisa and I have plans.'

Ha, well and truly dismissed. Lisa congratulated herself on resisting the urge to high-five Nathan with gratitude.

'Message received loud and clear.' Sam spun on the balls of her feet and headed off to the bathroom.

Lisa looked at Nathan, eyebrows raised. 'Well, she's—'

'A bit much, right? I'm sorry. I just felt bad about the boiler.'

Lisa smiled, determined to sustain her calm façade – maybe Dom's superpower had its merits after all. She followed Nathan to the kitchen. She could see a chicken and potatoes in the oven and registered the smell of the roast dinner for the first time. Even the thought of attempting to eat it made her feel sick, or perhaps it was the after-effect of discovering the naked woman in her boyfriend's flat. Lisa took a breath, but then realised she could perhaps use the latter to her advantage. 'OK … so as I'm being so very forgiving about the naked woman in your flat—'

'Woah, she—' Nathan interrupted.

But Lisa continued, 'You're going to have to forgive me, too.'

Nathan paused, tea towel in hand, crouched at the oven, as he looked at Lisa. 'I am? Why?'

'I've already eaten.'

Nathan opened the oven. The fat sizzled around the crispy potatoes, and a plume of smoke rolled to the ceiling, adding more heat to the temperature of the small kitchen. 'Really?'

'Yes … with Dom.'

'You ate with Dom?' Nathan raised his eyebrows.

'Yes, with Dom and Jack. We went to the pub and had roast. I'm sorry.' Lisa knew Nathan wasn't the jealous type, but her stomach couldn't help but twist. Ben would have been furious. Not that she would have been in the situation; having friends, going out for dinner with anybody other than Ben – they were things that didn't happen when she lived in London.

Nathan shut the oven door and leaned back against the sink with his arms folded, clearly a bit put out.

'You cancelled lunch,' Lisa offered.

'I postponed dinner.'

Lisa walked over to him. Reminding herself of Dom's words, she took a breath. 'I'm sorry. I just missed your message until it was too late. You can have yours today, and we can heat mine up tomorrow.' She looked at the vegetables in the steamer on the hob. 'You've cooked loads; there'll probably be enough for us both tomorrow. It will easily serve three.' As the words slipped out, she hoped she hadn't given him an idea that involved inviting Sam to stay for food.

'I suppose.'

'And I'm certainly up for dessert.' Lisa smiled, pressing herself against him.

'Oh, you are, are you?' Nathan feigned disinterest. 'Well, I'm not sure I fancy dessert now.'

Lisa grinned, recognising his playful tone. 'Oh really? Only I thought as you'd gone to so much trouble, I'd sort something special.'

Nathan looked at her, a sparkle in his eyes. 'How special?'

'Hmm, I don't know?' Lisa stroked her hand down his chest while she began kissing his neck, working her way up to his ear before whispering, 'Special enough.' She slipped her hand under his T-shirt, feeling his muscles flex at her touch.

'Ah hum.'

Lisa turned, her cheeks reddening as she registered Sam in the doorway.

Nathan coughed and pushed away from the side before turning off the heat on the hob. 'All done?'

'Yes, thanks. I—'

'I'll see you out, then,' Lisa interrupted. She turned to smile at Nathan, who gave her a knowing grin before she escorted Sam to the door. Determined not to feel intimidated by the woman before her who, even now fully dressed in jeans and a jumper, still looked stunning, Lisa attempted to maintain a smile. 'How long are you here for?'

'I'm not sure; it depends how things work out.'

Things? Lisa decided not to ask what things she was referring to for fear of the answer.

'It'll be good for Alex and me to be settled for a bit.'

'And Alex is your—'

'Oh, Uno!'

Nathan's tabby cat thudded down from his favourite position on the window seat and ran towards Sam, purring.

'I've missed you too.' She crouched to greet him.

Lisa felt a stab of jealousy, only for it to be replaced with elation as Uno ran past Sam, straight towards her, his purrs increasing and his tail flicking as he rubbed himself against her legs. Trying not to cheer out loud, and to curtail the grin that wanted to spread across her face, Lisa scooped Uno into her arms, grateful for his solidarity. 'Hello, you.' She rubbed behind his ears before looking at Sam, a smile tugging at her lips.

Walking towards the door, Sam paused to give Uno a stroke and met Lisa's gaze. 'He's my son.'

Discombobulated, Lisa frowned; surely she didn't mean the cat?

'Alex. He's my son. I'm surprised Nate didn't mention—'

Nate, again. 'No, he—'

'Especially as he delivered him.'

Chapter Four

Of all the days for Pete to be able to be around for the school and nursery run, Felicity couldn't believe it was the day she planned to root around in her cupboard for a pregnancy test. She was sure she had one in there somewhere, and if Pete had left at his usual time, she could have got it done first thing. Having been awake for most of the night, her mind was completely distracted.

Megan had managed to secure a chocolate biscuit and a Smarties yoghurt in her lunch by asking when Felicity wasn't paying attention – a sugar overload no-no on any normal day – and Callum had almost got away with taking his new Spiderman web slingers in his bag before she came to her senses. Not only had she recently purchased the refill can of ridiculously overpriced silly string, but she could imagine the call from the school after he had caused classroom chaos with it.

Stay focused on the children, Felicity! She knew they had a knack of knowing when her guard was down, so long as she could focus on getting them all out of the door, then she could take the test and rid her mind of the ridiculous thoughts of being pregnant. *Pregnant.* She really didn't want to be pregnant. *No. Don't let your mind go there. Focus on the children!*

'So is that OK, then? Only I thought it would be an issue, but if you're good with it, that'll be great.' Pete looked at Felicity expectantly.

Good with what? 'Umm.'

'Mummy, my zip's stuck.'

Felicity turned her attention to Callum, who was

standing before her with the two halves of the front of his coat connected at jaunty angles. 'Oh, Pumpkin, what have you done?' She tugged and wiggled at the zip, attempting to extract the lining firmly jammed in it.

'I did my shoes, Mummy. Mummy, my shoes!' Fred ran in from the hallway and wiggled his feet at Felicity.

'Wow! What a clever boy.' Felicity gave Fred a high-five, not having the heart to tell him his shoes were on the wrong feet, not when he'd actually found a matching pair and got them on without being asked. That was progress.

Pete glanced at Fred's feet, cocked his head and looked at Felicity quizzically.

Felicity shrugged. 'He'll be taking them off when he gets to nursery.' They could start working on which shoe went on which foot tomorrow. With a final tug, the lining came free from Callum's zip and Felicity stood up. 'Ta-dah!'

'Are we done?'

'You're missing one.'

Pete bellowed for Alice, whose footsteps were heard running from her room in response.

Having assembled all the children at the door, completed a final coat and bag check and given Felicity a kiss and an unexpected wink, Pete and all of the children left the house. As she watched the car leave the driveway, Felicity breathed a sigh. The house felt still and silent. It looked like the Tasmanian Devil had spun through it, but the peace was welcome. She went to the kitchen, drank a glass of water and tidied the breakfast things into the dishwasher. Now the opportunity was hers to take, she was hesitant about going upstairs and doing the test. Not knowing was filling her mind with fears, but knowing ... what would she do if the test were positive? She put the kettle on, attempting to push the fears away. *Pete has had a vasectomy, for goodness'*

25

sake. Is it even possible to get pregnant after your husband's had a vasectomy?

She picked up her phone and decided to Google it. The wisdom of Dr Google was normally something she tried to avoid. But this was statistical; there had to be facts. Facts based on sound evidence; facts that could dispel her fears. She typed 'Pregnancy after vasectomy'. The initial result was reassuring, stating that having a vasectomy was one of the best ways to prevent pregnancy. Felicity got a mug from the cupboard while still scrolling. Clicking a link that asked if vasectomy was one hundred per cent safe, Felicity's eyes went wide as she read, 'Only total abstinence is one hundred per cent effective. While rare, it has been known for sperm to travel across the void between the two blocked ends of the vas deferens. While the failure rate of vasectomy is very low, the possibility of becoming pregnant is there.'

'What the f—'

Her phone rang as she held it in her hand, making her jump. It was Lisa; Felicity decided not to answer. If she spoke to her, Lisa would know something was wrong, and Flick wasn't sure she would be able to avoid blurting out the thing utmost in her mind. While she had sent Lisa a text in her turmoil the day before, hoping to chat, she had soon realised it would be thoughtless to share her fears with her. How could she expect Lisa to understand that being pregnant would be the last thing she would want right now; that four babies was plenty? Two girls and two boys, their different personalities and cheeky ways meaning she had experienced all that bringing up a baby could offer. She did not need to do it again. Her desire to have babies had gone – she loved her children very much, but another? Could she love it too? How could she share those fears with anyone else when she hated herself for letting them enter her mind?

She left her phone on the kitchen side next to the hot kettle and empty mug and went upstairs.

Felicity rummaged in the bottom of her wardrobe. She was sure she had a pregnancy test in there somewhere. She found a bag containing a pile of clothes she intended to take to the charity shop. There was also some old, now slightly squashed sandals and two cushions she used to put on the bed until she realised life was too short to spend it taking decorative cushions on and off the bed. She swept her hand around the back of a box of photographs and didn't stop to look at Fred's birth cards, still in a gift bag where she had stored them, waiting for her to put them away in his memory chest.

'Aha!' She felt a cardboard box and pulled it free. Sure enough, it was a pregnancy test, the own-brand variety, but it would do the job. *Bugger!* It was out of date. She knew it must be around three years old. She had purchased a two-pack when she was pregnant with Fred so she would have one ready in case she had done the first too early. She hadn't needed the second test. The positive line had shown clearly in the window. Fred had been a surprise, but with Pete on the waiting list for his vasectomy at the time, it seemed as if it was meant to be; a brother for Callum before it was too late.

Determined to give the test a try despite it being out of date, Felicity went to the bathroom, opened the packet and read the instructions. She looked at herself in the mirror. *Please be negative.* She took off her watch so she could time it accurately. Crouched over the toilet, she readied herself. Hearing the front door open, her heart leapt and she almost dropped the test.

'Flick!'

Oh God! Oh no!

'Flick, you upstairs?'

Felicity heard Pete running up the stairs and glanced to check she had locked the door.

'Yes. Won't be long. I wasn't expecting you back.'

'I know, I thought I'd surprise you.'

Felicity stood, knickers and jeans at her ankles, bottom hovering above the toilet, and pregnancy test poised at the ready with her unknowing husband at the door. 'I just need a minute.' She looked again at the instructions resting on the bin and turned them over. *A minute? Two minutes? Arghhh, which was it?* 'Kids go in OK?' She tried to keep her voice even.

'All good, and thanks to a mix-up with that decking delivery I'm waiting on, I can't start work until eleven.'

Felicity could hear the mischief in his tone.

'So I thought what better way to fill that time than to come home and ravish my lovely wife.'

'Ha!' The words made her giggle despite her predicament. *Now? Really?* Felicity couldn't believe it. Pete was being spontaneous, sexy, funny and bloody lovely, and he couldn't have picked a worse time.

'So come on, wife, get yourself out here. Or shall I come in?'

She heard him touch the handle. *Please, don't open it!*

'No! I'm ... well ...' She needed to think of a distraction. 'You make us a tea and I'll be out by the time you're done.' Felicity wondered if she could have said anything less spontaneous and sexy if she tried.

'It's not quite the response I was after, but—'

'I've got one started,' she added, thinking Pete must think she had gone mad. Before their trip to Barbados, she had spent months attempting to spice up their love life, since then her appetite for sex had been insatiable, and now she was asking him to pop and make her a cup of tea when he was standing at the bathroom door offering to ravish her.

'OK.'

She heard Pete's footsteps disappear downstairs and attempted to relax enough to do the test. Thanking the fact she had drunk a glass of water, she put the cap on the stick and washed her hands. One minute. One minute was all she needed. The hands of her watch seemed to move painstakingly slowly. While she waited for the minute to tick by, she straightened her clothes, looked at herself in the mirror, brushed her hair and rooted through the bin for a way to hide the evidence.

As a minute was up, she braced herself and looked.

Oh God! The air escaped her. 'Now what?' She looked back at the instructions, comparing the result to the pictures. She tried tilting her head and squinting.

'Right, I'm back.'

Felicity jumped at the sound of Pete's voice.

'Your tea is here, and if you don't get out here, then I'm definitely coming in!'

She hurriedly put the test and instructions back in the box. She took the lid off the empty shampoo bottle she'd found and squashed all of the evidence inside before putting it back in the bin. She washed her hands and opened the door. Her mind was a muddle, but there was nothing she could do right now. Her head already hurt from overthinking everything through the night. She took a breath.

Pete was standing before her, he was wearing his work boots – a thing she'd normally complain about him doing indoors – but with his well-worn work jeans and muscle-hugging T-shirt, the overall look was bloody sexy. The desire she saw in his eyes made her smile as he tugged her closer. Wrapping his arms around her, his lips met hers, and all thoughts of the test slipped from her mind.

Kissing, properly kissing, was something they'd rediscovered in Barbados. Before that, it had been a long time since Felicity had felt the desire that spread through her body when she was thoroughly kissed. Feeling the hunger in the kisses from the man she loved, his need for her becoming more urgent as his tongue explored her mouth, was something she'd missed without even knowing it. She had forgotten how it awoke feelings deep inside. How it caused her body to react.

Pete walked her, still in his arms, through to the bedroom, and she could feel how much she wanted him – needed him. As the backs of her legs reached the bed, they paused. Pete stepped back, and she missed the feel of his lips on hers and his arms around her. He smiled, a wicked smile, the glint in his darkened eyes clear as he traced his hands down her body, brushing over her breasts, causing her to want more. His hands moved to her jeans while he kissed gently around her neck before making his kisses deeper. She tipped her head back and moved her hands round his back, feeling the flex in his firm muscles honed from manual labour. Goosebumps spread across her enlivened body.

Over his shoulder, Felicity spotted her ransacked wardrobe still open. She closed her eyes, not wanting any distractions. Her breathing grew deeper, and the rise and fall of her chest as Pete undid her jeans and slid his hands to her bottom made her breasts strain at the material of her bra and ache to be touched. He stooped to remove her jeans before sliding his hands upwards and removing her T-shirt; the teasing brush of his hands on her body caused a groan to escape her.

Pete met her gaze and offered a wickedly promise-filled

smile before tracing kisses down her body. She moved her hands into his auburn hair, tugging as desire took hold of her and she felt her need for him increase. Standing on shaky legs, she luxuriated in the touch of his mouth on her body.

Sliding back on to and up the bed, she tugged his clothes, pulling him with her as she removed his T-shirt at the same time. Deftly she undid his jeans as her legs wrapped round him. She heard his boots thud to the floor. Feeling the weight of him pressed against her urged her to want more. To feel him closer. Deeper. All of him. She felt his breathing grow ragged. Her mind was lost to him and the moment. It didn't matter what the test said, it didn't matter what the future held, the only thing that mattered was the fact she loved Pete Willis and at that very moment in time he was causing sensations to cascade wildly through her body.

As they lay, sometime later, side by side on the bed, their breathing recovering, Pete wrapped Felicity in his arms and kissed the top of her head. 'Do you feel thoroughly ravished, wife?'

Felicity laughed. 'I do.' She leaned up on his chest and looked into his eyes. 'But I am regretting letting you watch *Poldark* with me. Ravished! What are you like?'

Pete laughed and kissed her again before grabbing Felicity's arm and looking at her watch. 'Bugger me, look at the time.'

'What? Are you late?' Felicity sat up as Pete moved down the bed, pulling his clothes back on.

'It's not that. Mum's coming. She's being dropped off. She'll be here any minute.'

'What? Why?'

Pete wrestled his way back in to his T-shirt. 'To stay.'

'What?' Felicity felt the warm afterglow of sex dissipate as quickly as if somebody had thrown a bucket of ice water over her.

'I asked you this morning.' Pete looked at her, confused. 'It's not for long.'

Felicity recalled the half a conversation she'd had with Pete while struggling with Callum's zip. 'That's what you were talking about? Your mother coming to stay?'

'Yes. And you said you were good with it.'

'Of course I didn't. I had no bloody idea what you were on about.'

'But you said—'

'I didn't say yes, your mother could bloody come and stay.'

'But you didn't say no, either.'

Felicity flopped back on the bed, pulled the quilt over herself and put the pillow over her face in an attempt not to scream or cry or both. Her day was swinging from extremes: fear, dread, anxiety, pure pleasure, and now ... now she was faced with doom – in the shape of a sixty-something-year-old woman who found fault with almost everything she did.

'With her ankle still not right, it's the least we can do. Anyway, I should be able to help get her settled before I go to work. She's bringing that fold-out bed thing she's got, so she won't be any hassle.'

Felicity peered out from under her pillow. 'Isn't mentioning your mother and no hassle in the same sentence an oxymoron or something?'

Pete sat on the edge of the bed and rested his hand on Felicity's leg. 'Flick, I could hardly say no.'

Despite the fact Sue had broken her ankle after treading on Lego left on the stairs in their house on Boxing Day, Felicity knew she and Pete had got off lightly when it came to nursing duties. Driving Sue to physiotherapy a couple of times was nothing compared to having her to stay and being at her constant beck and call, as Pete's sister had. Felicity flopped the pillow back on to her face, muffling her voice. 'Is your sister finally ready to kill her?'

'No, she just needs a little, umm, respite—'

A ring at the doorbell made Felicity spring up from the bed and start grabbing her clothes. Pete laughed at her predicament as he held up her bra.

'Oh my god, your mother is here! I'm naked and the house ... the house is a bloody tip. All I did was throw the breakfast things in the dishwasher.'

Pete picked up the two cold mugs of tea from the bedside table. 'I'll make fresh ones, shall I?'

Chapter Five

'How did it go?'

Sitting in her van, Lisa read Dom's message and typed: 'All good. Doc McFluffins was a gent. I still have ten fingers. You can stand down.'

'Not with the rabbit but good to know you won't need my medical services. I meant with Nathan,' came the reply.

Lisa bit her lip. She had known what Dom was asking, but despite the fact it had been a few days, she didn't have anything to report. She sighed flatly and decided to go for honesty: 'It hasn't, or didn't. A bit of an odd story involving an almost naked woman and the fact my boyfriend delivered her baby!'

'What? On Sunday night?'

'Yes to the naked woman. No to the delivery – that was before.'

With that her phone rang, and Dom's name flashed on to the screen. Lisa answered straight away.

'Are you being deliberately obscure? What's going on?'

Lisa welcomed his call and the concern in his voice. She explained about how she had discovered Sam wrapped in a towel in Nathan's flat and about what Sam had said about Nathan delivering her son.

When she finished, Dom let out a breath and an expletive before readopting his concerned tone. 'And what did Nathan say about that?'

'I told you her boiler was broken.'

'No, about delivering her baby.'

'I didn't ask him about it. I figured if he wanted to tell me, he would.'

'It's not an easy thing to just bring up, though, is it?

"By the way, that woman you just found naked in my flat, I delivered her son." Telling your other half you've seen someone else's foof is never an easy conversation.'

'Foof?' Lisa laughed.

'Yes, foof. No matter what the circumstances of seeing it, partners don't respond well. Believe me.'

'Maybe that's because you called it a foof?' Lisa giggled, grateful that Dom was able to make her smile about the situation.

'Really? Do you think that's why I never truly hit it off with women?'

'That and the fact you never found one to match up to your Leonardo DiCaprio crush.' Lisa laughed.

'Good point.' Dom paused before making his tone more serious. 'Don't use what that woman, Sam, said as an excuse not to have your conversation though, will you? Make sure you say what you need to say.'

'I won't.'

'Won't use it as an excuse, or won't say what you need to say?'

'Ha, I won't use it as an excuse.'

'Oh well, that was a noncommittal tone if ever I heard one.'

Lisa coughed, deepening her voice. 'Seriously, I won't use it as an excuse.'

Dom copied her tone. 'Good, so I'll ring again to check tomorrow—'

'But—'

'Do it, Rose, you know it makes sense.'

Lisa softened at the mention of Dom's nickname for her. He called her Rose partly because she was repeatedly calling for Jack – his gran's Labrador – when they first met; but also, as Lisa liked to point out to him, because he had a far greater knowledge of the film *Titanic* than was appropriate for a thirty-two-year-old, single man.

'I will,' she promised, not feeling the conviction of her words. 'But right now I need to feed these kittens.' Lisa glanced over at the house to see Kit and Kaboodle, or Kit and Boo as she liked to call them when their owners weren't around, looking at her expectantly from the lounge windowsill.

As Lisa opened the front door, the kittens, who hadn't yet grown into their long legs and big ears, ran from the living room to greet her. Lisa smiled and put her phone and keys down in readiness to say a proper hello, but before she could speak, the pungent and distinctive smell of cat poo hit the back of her throat. She gagged and put her hand over her nose and mouth. For two such innocent-looking kittens, they could create an incredible stench. Glancing towards the kitchen, Lisa spotted the offending aimed at and missed litter-tray disaster.

She retched, grabbed a scarf she saw hanging on the banister, and wrapped it round her nose and mouth so as to free her hand. Encouraging the kittens into the living room with the aid of a feather-covered ball on the end of a string, Lisa shut the door; the clean-up operation would be easier without their help. 'Right!' Once in the kitchen, she opened the window and back door before sourcing appropriate cleaning products. Finally, snapping on the Marigold gloves she'd found next to the sink, she was ready. Catching a glimpse of herself in the reflection of the window, she rolled her eyes and hoped nobody would come home to find her looking like a cat-poo-cleaning ninja.

When she finished, Lisa placed the black sack in the outside bin and lowered the scarf from her face before taking a few much-needed cleansing breaths. As she did so, she made a mental note to get together a tool kit of disposable gloves, pet-friendly disinfectant, bin bags, kitchen roll, air freshener and disposable face masks. She had been lucky this time the house had been well stocked, but what if it hadn't? As it was, she was going to have to explain the missing Marigold gloves from the kitchen sink.

Locking the back door, Lisa called to the kittens and went to free them from the lounge. They bolted excitedly to the kitchen. Thankfully, they hadn't caused any devastation in the time she had left them, and for a moment at least they were still – both in one place crunching their way through their kibble. She hoped that by the time they needed their litter tray again, it wouldn't be on her watch.

Deciding now would be a good time to write a note for their owners, Lisa took out her Purrfect Pet Sitter notebook from her bag and rummaged for her pen. With her hand slipping into all the corners of her rucksack, she remembered taking the pen out and using it in the van to note down a new contact. She scanned the kitchen side but couldn't find one. 'Ah ha!' She had more luck in the living room and sat to write a note explaining about the clear-up and the now missing Marigolds – which she offered to pay for.

Leaving the note next to the kettle, she spotted Kit steadily munching his way through Kaboodle's bowl of food. 'Hey, pickle, that's your sister's. How come she's letting you get away with that?'

Lisa called Boo and looked around for her. She checked behind the fridge – a previous hiding place from which she had been recovered – but couldn't find her. Spotting the still-open window, her heart thudded and she swore. 'Oh no, no, no, no, Boo, you wouldn't.' As she went to look into the garden, Lisa hoped, truly hoped, that Boo hadn't somehow managed to clamber out. The kittens were twelve weeks old, they'd recently had their second injections, but their owner had given strict instructions that they were to be kept in until fourteen weeks. And then, quite rightly, she wanted to be the one to take them out.

Lisa swallowed as she looked across the lawn to see Boo almost grinning back at her. Not wanting Kit to follow suit, Lisa scooped him up. His slender frame and soft fur made him feel vulnerable in her hands and caused Lisa's fear for his sister to increase. Popping him into the living room, Lisa gave him a quick reassuring stroke before taking a breath and heading back to the kitchen.

Opening the back door, Lisa shook the box of kibble and called Kaboodle. Perhaps if she hadn't just eaten all she wanted of her food, it would have been harder to resist. But as it was, the lure of the great outdoors and the taste of freedom were more appealing. Stuffing a handful of the kibble in her pocket and leaving the box on the floor, Lisa walked slowly towards the escapee, keeping her voice calm and even despite the panic she could feel growing inside.

Boo was edging stealthily through the grass, her movements slow and precise. With her legs bent and her tail held straight and low, she looked every bit the lioness ready to strike. Boo was feisty and determined to have her fun, but unlike her formidable feline cousin, she was small and unaware of the dangers of the big wide world; Lisa knew she couldn't let anything happen to her. The object of her prey, as far as Lisa could see, was the long grass at the base of an old sycamore tree. Caught every now and then by the breeze, the movement of the grass seemed to fascinate the inquisitive cat.

As Lisa wondered if she could just make a grab for Boo while her attention was elsewhere, the kitten pounced; taking a leap into the air, she landed on the grass, but as she did so, a squirrel darted out of hiding and began scampering up the tree, spiralling the trunk as it went. Kaboodle, at first startled, recovered all too quickly for a kitten on her first outdoor adventure and began to give chase.

'Oh no! Kaboodle, don't you do that.' Lisa dashed for the tree, but it was no good; the spritely kitten was out of reach. Even if she jumped, Lisa couldn't reach her. And still Boo was climbing higher, lured by the squirrel, who was now leaping from branch to branch in an acrobatic display Lisa truly hoped Boo wouldn't attempt to copy. Trying again to get the kitten's attention, Lisa called her and held out the food. But still, the determined kitten ignored her. Lisa looked around the garden for a ladder and peered in the shed window, but couldn't see one.

Returning to the tree, she could see Boo teetering on a branch. The squirrel was nowhere to be seen and had probably made an escape into the trees behind the garden. Lisa was grateful Boo hadn't followed there; it led to fields and a train line beyond.

With the object of Kaboodle's focus gone, she seemed to notice for the first time that she was about fifteen feet off the ground. As if to tell Lisa about her predicament, the kitten started meowing loudly. Lisa spoke to her, reassuring her, as she attempted to encourage her down, but instead of making a move to return to the ground, the kitten's calls became more desperate. Lisa really didn't want Boo to fall and injure herself.

Testing the lowest branch with a tug, Lisa decided there was only one thing for it; she'd have to climb the tree and help Kaboodle down. Deciding the branch might just be strong enough, she looked for a sturdy foothold in the bark. Her jeans were a bit tighter than she'd have chosen if she'd known she was going to be scaling a tree, but needs must.

At least she was grateful to be wearing her trainers instead of her walking boots.

Grabbing the lower branch with one hand, she put her left arm around the trunk. With one foot on a gnarly piece of bark, she pushed up. 'Here goes!' Lisa had climbed trees when she was younger. It had seemed easy then, when she had been desperate to get higher than her brother, Luke, and to prove that she was the best. Looking up at the tree, its branches reaching into the sky overhead, Lisa reminded herself that being at least fifteen years older should simply mean she was stronger – *not more of a coward, more aware of the dangers and oh so much less supple*. The fear she could feel inside was, she told herself, unnecessary; she just wasn't sure how to convince her shaking legs of that fact. *Come on, Lisa, you can do this!*

Spurred on by the desperation in Kaboodle's meowing, Lisa hauled herself upwards, staying as close as she could to the trunk. 'Look for the branches about the size of your wrist,' she remembered her dad saying. Wise words, sound advice that had stayed with her, locked in her sub-conscious, for a tree-climbing occasion to occur; now that occasion was here, and she was balancing on a branch half the size of her wrist, six feet off the ground, she wished the wise words had stayed locked away.

Lisa attempted to keep her voice even and to keep reassuring Kaboodle as she pulled herself ever closer to her. Determined not to look down, she focused on the next branch, the next foothold and the sorry-for-herself kitten, whose first outdoor adventure had gone so very wrong. 'Nearly there, Boo. One more branch and I'll be with you.' As Lisa, still remaining close to the trunk, pulled herself up level with the kitten, she realised she hadn't thought this through. How could she get Kaboodle off her branch and safely down? If she still had the scarf on, she could have wrapped her in it or made a sling to carry her down. But she didn't. Lisa knew she would definitely need both hands free to make the descent.

Pondering how else she could make a sling, Lisa wondered if her T-shirt would work. As she tried to decide if she would be able to take it off safely and if she wanted to risk being arrested for being up a tree in her bra and jeans, in what was a quite nice neighbourhood not far from her mum's house, Kaboodle began to walk towards her. Dismissing all plans to fashion a sling, Lisa wedged her back against the tree and opened her arms for the kitten, who ran the final stretch with wide eyes. Lisa scooped her into her hands, welcoming the feel of her soft sable fur and feeling the vulnerability of her slight body. In order to keep a safe hold of her, Lisa moved Kaboodle closer and wrapped her in her arms. Despite the fact they were still in a tree and a long way from the ground, Lisa felt relieved that Kaboodle was safe. But with no way to get the kitten down and telephoning for help being out of the question, as she had left her phone in the house, Lisa realised she would have to sit it out in the tree until the kittens' owner returned home. A glance at her watch and the stiffness creeping into her limbs made her question how feasible a plan that was. Building her voice up slowly so as not to frighten the kitten, Lisa decided to call for help. Once her voice reached a reasonable level, she watched the windows of the surrounding houses. Nothing. Not a single curtain twitched.

About to give up and accept her fate, Lisa saw the garden gate swing open. While she couldn't believe who was standing there, she knew at least a rescue was about to be co-ordinated and that it would be carried out with military precision.

'Harold. Mr Martin. It's good to see you.' While Lisa didn't always find it good to see her mum's ex-military, elderly neighbour, there was no doubt she was relieved to see him now.

Walking purposefully towards the tree, Harold looked at Lisa and called, 'Spotted you from the fields. I've telephoned for reinforcements.'

'The fields? But ...' Lisa paused, deciding to leave the many questions in her head for when she and Kaboodle were safely back on the ground. After a long career in the army, Harold Martin had found his calling in retirement as head of the neighbourhood watch. He was also a keen observer of nature and a birdwatcher. Lisa hoped the latter explained the binoculars hanging round his neck, as opposed to him taking his neighbourhood-watch duties a tad too far.

'Should be here any minute. We'll soon have you down.'

The words were reassuring. 'Not long now, Boo, did you hear? Help is on its way.' About to ask what Harold's plan was, Lisa became aware of a siren drawing closer; from her vantage point in the tree she could also see flashing blue lights, flashing blue lights that had turned into the street and come to a halt outside the house. She hadn't met the members of Nathan's watch, but she had more than a suspicion she was about to. *Thank goodness I kept my top on!* Her cheeks turned red and she looked down at Kaboodle.

'Oh, Boo, I think you're about to become a cliché.'

Chapter Six

'You have to admit "Firefighter Rescues Girlfriend From Cat-astrophy!" is a good headline.' Felicity held up a copy of the *Gazette* and grinned at Lisa across the table.

'I can't believe you brought that with you. This is supposed to be a night out to escape the traumas of last week.'

'I didn't, it was on the newspaper rack by the door.'

Lisa took the paper and laid it on the table in front of her. 'Firstly, what kind of bar has a newspaper rack, and secondly, how much of a slow news week is it to have this story on the front page?'

Felicity laughed. 'Welcome to Cin Cin, you must be used to this whole café-meets-bar vibe by now. And as for a slow news week, it's the *Gazette*; firefighter rescues a woman who was rescuing a cat is hot news for them!'

'You're not funny. It was mortifying. I am perfectly capable of climbing back down a tree from that height. I just can't do it holding a kitten.'

'Hmm, well, it says right there' – Felicity leaned over and pointed at a paragraph in the article – 'after they'd rescued Kaboodle, you needed rescuing too; ladders, ropes and a harness are mentioned.' Felicity giggled and picked up her orange juice.

'My bloody arms were dead and my legs had turned to jelly. I'd been holding Boo and concentrating so hard on keeping her safe I hadn't dared move.'

'I'm sure. And needing to be rescued had nothing to do with the fact Nathan was there, in uniform, ready to throw you over his shoulder and carry you down to safety.'

'Seriously? With that imagination you should write for the *Gazette*. That is most certainly not how it happened. Believe me, it was a whole lot less glamorous.'

'Oh, don't shatter my illusions.' Felicity screwed up her nose and turned the newspaper back to face her. 'It was a bit sexy though, wasn't it? I mean, look at Nathan holding the kitten. That's calendar-worthy photography right there.'

Lisa put her head to one side as she studied the picture on the front of the newspaper, and her cheeks turned red.

Felicity giggled. 'Oh my God, it was sexy, wasn't it?'

'OK, it was a bit sexy, but it was still mortifying.' Lisa took a sip of her wine as thoughts flooded her mind about the evening she and Nathan had spent together after the rescue, when she couldn't keep her hands off him. Feeling her hot flush spread to her neck, she decided to change the subject. 'In other news ... how is the mother-in-law? Sue driven you crazy yet?'

'I thought you said we were here to escape the traumas of the week!'

'Been that good, has it?'

As Pete knew the owners of Cin Cin, Felicity glanced around ensuring they weren't within earshot before speaking, 'It's just such bad timing. Pete and I, we were just finding our rhythm again, making a bit of time for us now the children are getting older, but with Sue staying, that's gone out of the window. And, to be honest, I just don't know how Pete's sister has coped. I mean, Sue tries to be nice, I think, but it's how she goes about it. She keeps insisting on helping round the house but does it in a way that seems like she's suggesting my way isn't good enough, and then there are the things she says.'

'Like?'

'Like, "You look nice ... today"!'

'Oh.' Lisa grimaced.

'Or "Megan's hair looks so lovely … after a shower"; honestly why not just say the nice bit?'

'You should speak to her in the same way, use a Sueism; maybe she'll pick up on it and realise what she's doing.'

'That would be good. But maybe I'm just being too sensitive. I've been all over the place this week and …' Felicity wiped away the tears welling in her eyes.

Lisa put down her glass. 'Flick, what is it? What's wrong?'

Felicity took a shaky breath. 'I don't know. I probably just need a distraction, to get out of the house more—'

'Oh, Flick, I'm so sorry.' Lisa felt a swell of guilt wash over her.

'Why? It's not your fault.'

'But it is. I know you want to go running again, and I haven't sorted a time with you.'

'It's fine. I know you're busy. I didn't mean—'

'But I'm not too busy, not really. I'm just horrible—'

'Horrible? Why?' Felicity looked at Lisa, a frown reflecting her confusion.

'Because I should have been a better friend and just said—'

'Said what?'

Lisa picked up her wine and took a drink before meeting Felicity's eyes. 'I hate running.'

Felicity began to giggle at Lisa's confession.

'No, I'm serious. I mean really hate it. It's just not for me. I'm sorry … Don't laugh.'

Felicity attempted to compose herself in readiness to speak. 'Sorry … I mean I'm not. But, Lisa, you don't have to come running with me. Why didn't you just say? I don't mind going alone – I actually went out for a short run the other evening.'

'Oh, Flick, I—'

'Lisa, it doesn't matter. Running is something I want to do; it really doesn't matter if you don't want to come too. I want to do it, for me.'

'But I thought—'

'What? That I wouldn't be your friend if you didn't run with me? We're not at school any more.'

'No. I thought … I thought I'd be letting you down. I'm here for you; you know that, don't you? No matter what.'

Felicity smiled. 'I do, really I do. But you don't have to do things you don't want to do to prove it, or to tiptoe round things to protect my feelings. God knows Pete did that enough after I lost Mum. Just say it how it is. That's what friends do.'

Lisa smiled. 'Honesty. I like that.' She lifted her glass. 'Here's to being there and being honest.'

Felicity raised her glass and drank down the rest of her orange juice.

Lisa put her drink down and smiled. 'You know, I could get a bike and ride along next to you. Maybe use one of those loudhailer things and encourage you along like a coxswain.'

'Bog off, I want to go running for peace!' Felicity's phone rang and she ignored it. 'You see, no peace, and that's what I really need.'

'Well, don't forget we have our birthday trip to France to look forward to. When we're away you can have all the peace you want. For the weekend anyway.'

'Yes. I can't wait. I'm looking forward to it so much. Not the turning-thirty part – I could do without that. But the holiday and the you, me and your parents' chalet for the weekend part. It sounds perfect. A year ago, I would never have imagined we'd be friends again and celebrating our thirtieth birthdays together.'

'Me either and now look at us. A birthday weekend planned, and our men joining us for the rest of the week after. Bliss!'

'Hmm, you have remembered Pete's bringing the children too, haven't you? Bliss might not be the word for it.'

'You know I love your children.'

'I hope you're still saying that after the week is up. And you're sure your mum knows we're all staying too? Only I remember, chaos and mess were never exactly her favourite things.'

'She is absolutely fine with it. She's mellowed a bit since we were younger, and besides, she'll be back in England, so what she doesn't know won't hurt her.' Lisa laughed.

Felicity's phone rang, again. 'Honestly, you'd think Pete could cope without calling.' She rolled her eyes picking up the call as it went to voicemail.

Lisa watched as the colour drained from her friend's cheeks. 'Flick, what is it?'

'It's Sue.'

'Is she OK?'

'She won't be. I'm going to bloody kill her.'

Chapter Seven

The house was too quiet. The children were all in bed, the television wasn't on and Pete didn't call out to her as he always did when she came in after him. Felicity slipped off her coat, put her keys in the basket and removed her shoes. She took a breath. Walking to the kitchen, she realised she was shaking; she wasn't sure if it was because she was angry with Sue, or cross at herself for not sorting the situation out before now. As she opened the door, she saw Pete standing at the kettle, and Sue with a smug look on her face sitting at the kitchen table. The bathroom bin was on the floor and the shampoo bottle and pregnancy test were on the table.

Sue manoeuvred herself to the back of her chair, to make herself taller, and folded her arms.

Pete turned, but didn't meet Felicity's gaze as he placed her mug of tea next to his on the table.

Felicity sat down; her heart was thumping. The whole situation reminded her of the day she'd had to tell her mum she was pregnant with Megan. She had been so scared, not because she didn't want her baby, she did. She knew that. But because she didn't want to let her mum down or for her to think badly of her; she had never wanted her daughter to be a young mum, yet there she was, not long with Pete, barely beyond being a teenager and pregnant. Felicity was pretty sure this situation wasn't going to turn out as positively as that had. She decided not to speak; if Sue and Pete had jumped to conclusions, she wanted to hear what they were.

Pete broke the silence. As he spoke Felicity heard the

tremor in his voice. 'Mum wanted to help. She said she would clean the bathroom. I know you hate doing it.'

Thanks for pointing that out in front of your mother, Pete.

'So I let her. She was emptying the bin and thought we should rinse out and recycle the plastic bottles.'

Of course she did.

Sue continued to sit silently. Felicity wondered what would come out of her mouth if Pete let her speak. She was chewing hard on her lip, obviously with something on her mind.

'She found that inside.' Pete gestured to the pregnancy test.

Felicity looked at it directly for the first time. *No line.* She noticed that Sue had cleaned off the remnants of shampoo from the bottle. Felicity imagined her wiping it, polishing the precious nugget of evidence she'd found ready to present it in a court in which she intended to be judge and jury.

Pete looked at Felicity, his eyes questioning. 'What does it mean?'

'I can tell you what it means,' Sue interjected.

Felicity gasped.

'Don't.' Pete glared at Sue, a warning, before taking a breath and looking back at Felicity.

'It means I thought … I mean … I think I might be pregnant.' Felicity looked into Pete's eyes, deciding to ignore Sue's presence. 'I didn't tell you because I didn't think it was possible.'

'I know a way it's possible.'

'Mum, that's enough.' Pete thudded his hand down onto the table. 'I told you you're wrong!'

'Really, Sue? Do you not know me at all? Do you really think I would cheat on Pete?' Felicity looked Sue in the eyes and held her gaze. Even though she had expected the insinuation, hearing the words still hurt.

Sue shrank at the question and coughed before speaking. 'He's had a vasectomy.' Her voice was less caustic now.

'Yes, he has. And vasectomies sometimes fail. Believe me, I've Googled it. A lot. In fact, one in two thousand vasectomies fail. There are lots of cases online, where it just didn't work, where the body heals itself, or where the sperm makes it across the space between the vas … vas … I don't know, the tubes or something.'

They all sat in silence for a moment.

Finally Pete spoke. 'And are you pregnant? What did the test show?'

'I don't know. I thought I saw a line, but it was pale, too pale. The test is out of date, and since your mum's been here, I haven't had the chance to buy another one or do it again.'

Pete leaned across the table and took Felicity's hand. She welcomed the gesture and the strength she always found from him.

'OK.' He smiled at Felicity, the tension having gone from his face, before turning to Sue. 'Best you get to bed now then, Mum. You've heard what you needed to hear. Now this is between Flick and me.'

Sue looked horrified to have been dismissed from the conversation, and for a moment Felicity wondered if she was going to protest; instead she meekly stood and made a show of gathering her crutches before turning.

'Aren't you forgetting something?' Pete asked.

Sue turned and looked questioningly.

Pete nodded towards Felicity.

'I'm sorry, Felicity, I am. I just saw the test and, well, I knew about Pete's vasectomy, and I thought about my son first. I didn't want to see him get hurt.'

Felicity cleared her throat. 'I can understand that.'

Sue turned to leave.

'Talking to me first …'

Sue paused, unspeaking.

Felicity continued, 'that would have been the way to stop anyone being hurt. I would have explained if you'd asked me.'

Sue nodded and pulled the door shut behind her.

Felicity let out a long steadying breath and smiled at Pete before he pulled her into a hug.

'You never thought I'd cheat on you, did you?'

'No. Not really. But I was scared. I mean, I was confused why you wouldn't tell me you were taking a pregnancy test.'

Felicity sank further into Pete's arms, wondering how to explain her feelings about the possibility of being pregnant. She fought back the tears that wanted to flow and took a breath. 'Sorry I didn't tell you. It's just … well … I needed a bit of time to get my head round the idea. I mean, we have four beautiful children. But another one? Seriously, Pete, what if I am pregnant … then what—'

'Then we're calling it Thor.'

'What?' Felicity sat up and looked at Pete's excited face. 'Are you mad? Why?'

'Because he's got superpowers. We thought we'd killed them all off—'

'All who off?'

'My swimmers, but no, Thor there' – Pete gestured to Felicity's stomach – 'he's made it through, against the odds.'

'Wouldn't that make him Aquaman?' The words came out of Felicity's mouth before she could stop them. She had no idea why she was being drawn in to this conversation.

Pete looked at her as if she were mad. 'You can't call a baby Aquaman, and you can't have an adult called Aquababy – see, it makes no sense.'

'But calling a baby Thor does?' Felicity wanted to point out that this whole conversation wasn't making any sense; she might not even be pregnant. *Please don't let me be pregnant.*

'Yes, because it works no matter what the age, and imagine how cool the others would think having a brother called Thor would be.'

'Megan would be mortified. Why am I being drawn into this? Pete, I might not even be pregnant.'

'But you think you could be?'

'Well, I've missed a period and I felt dizzy and, oh, I don't know, maybe I am imagining it all because of the missed period.'

'So let's do a test, then. One that isn't out of date.' He offered her a reassuring smile.

'Yes, we have to, I guess.' Felicity thought about all the cases she had scrolled through online. She had even ventured onto mums' forums – something she usually avoided due to never really feeling part of the clique and not knowing the meaning of all of the in-house abbreviations. On there she found threads where people were posing the same question. Too many of those who replied seemed to know someone who knew someone it had happened to. She felt an ache in her chest. Doing a test might put her mind at rest, and then she could put all of the fear and anxiety behind her. But what if it didn't? What if it confirmed a pregnancy?

'I'll go to Tesco, then.'

'Pete, it's almost ten o'clock.'

'It will still be open. Wouldn't you rather know for sure?'

Yes, no, arghh, maybe. 'Yes.'

'Then I'll go now.' Pete gave Felicity a kiss, took his keys from his pocket, and went to the door.

'Pete.'

He paused.

'I love you.'

'I love you too.'

'And, Pete. Get a digital one. I don't think I'll be able to cope with another maybe, maybe not situation.'

'Digital, got it.'

As Pete shut the door, Felicity leaned back against her chair. She should have known she could rely on him. He had managed to distract her from her fears with his nonsense about calling the baby Thor – *please let that be nonsense* – and then he had been calm, sensible and pragmatic. She looked at the clock; the sound of its ticking seemed louder than normal in the too-silent house. Pete's journey to the shop and back wouldn't take long. Felicity picked up her mug of tea and took a sip to calm her nerves. She wished it were something stronger. *It will be OK—* Felicity jumped from her thoughts as the kitchen door swung open.

Pete looked at her. 'Actually, will you go? I've got no idea where these things are, and you can bet it won't go through the self-service without some issue.'

Chapter Eight

Lisa hurried up the stairs, laden with a bag of shopping in each hand. She knew Nathan was visiting his parents and wanted to get everything ready before he was due back. As she passed Sam's door, it opened. Lisa turned to see a boy; he looked a little older than Flick's Megan. Maybe around ten, Lisa thought. His sandy-coloured fringe reached his deep blue eyes, and his cheeks were peppered with freckles. His jeans had designer holes at the knees and he was wearing a T-shirt with "Summer Surf Club" emblazoned across the front. Lisa smiled at him.

'Was it—' Sam appeared at the door, halting when she saw Lisa.

As Sam and the boy stood side by side, Lisa could see a resemblance between them and wondered if the boy was Alex. *Don't be stupid that would make Sam, what, fifteen, sixteen when she had him?* Lisa dismissed the thought.

'We wondered who it was.' Sam folded her arms.

The boy, clearly not interested in Lisa, offered a brief smile, shrugged and went back inside the flat.

'Just me.' *Just?* Lisa wished she hadn't used a diminutive term for herself.

'Best to be safe. I know Nate doesn't always lock his door.'

Lisa thought about the times she had been to Nathan's flat, the door was always locked, but she decided acquiescence was probably the quickest way to get upstairs and out of Sam's company. 'Good plan. I'm sure Nathan will appreciate it.' Lisa continued up the stairs.

'That's Nate, always appreciative.'

Oh, bog off! Lisa didn't want to let Sam annoy her, but there was something about every word that came out of her mouth that made Lisa think she had an ulterior motive. Rolling her eyes, she politely called back, 'He is indeed!'

Once in Nathan's flat and having put the shopping bags down, Lisa decided she was not going to let her encounter with Sam spoil her mission for the evening. Having decided tonight was the night for telling Nathan about her life in London and losing the baby with Ben, she just wanted to get on with it. After the rescue debacle she had put it off again, but, now it had been a month since she had spoken to Dom, he and Felicity were increasingly on her case, and she knew herself that putting it off was silly. The baby she had lost, her little Pip, was a part of who she was. She needed Nathan to know that. She wanted the evening to be perfect and had it all planned out in her head. Dom had told her that taking control of the situation was the best approach. That it would allow her to take it at her pace, to remain calm and to remember that Nathan loved her.

Lisa had teased that Dom was turning into his gran, with his words of wisdom, but then again she knew Winnie would have put it more bluntly than that; her advice was always direct and generally apt. Lisa couldn't wait to see her again; the thought of her walk with Jack pencilled in her diary for the following afternoon made her smile.

Lisa decided pork chops, apple sauce, mashed potato, steamed baby veg and gravy was perfect for her meal with Nathan. It didn't take long to prepare and – with its association of being a classic in the Blake household – it was comfort food. She had considered doing dauphinoise potatoes, but the potential for error was too high when she needed everything to go right. For dessert she had bought a tub of rocky road ice cream – Nathan's favourite. Along with unpacking the shopping, she popped a bottle of wine in the fridge and fed and made a fuss of Uno.

When she finally heard Nathan come in, she felt her stomach flip and wondered if a meal was such a good idea to accompany this conversation.

'Wow, that smells good.' Nathan walked into the kitchen, stood behind Lisa and slid his arms around her waist.

She felt the fine stubble of his chin brush her neck as he kissed her there. *No turning back now.* 'It will be ready in about ten minutes. There's wine in the fridge.'

Nathan kissed her again. 'Careful, I could get used to this.'

'You might not say that after you've eaten it.' Lisa laughed. Generally Nathan cooked for them, and Lisa organised takeaway, but she felt that didn't have the same I've-made-an-effort-for-you touch when it came to preparing a special meal.

'Well, it looks good to me, and if you've got it all under control, I'll go and shower.'

'Sure.' Lisa exhaled as Nathan left the room. She thought she had everything under control, but now Nathan was home, she could feel nerves growing inside. *Come on, Lisa, hold it together!*

With the chops hissing and spitting under the grill, Lisa put the veg in the steamer and remembered the apple sauce. First of all searching for it and then staring into the fridge, Lisa couldn't find it. Come to think of it, she didn't remember putting it in there as she had unpacked the shopping. Pondering whether she had left it at the shop, she began to wonder if she had actually picked it up off the shelf. She remembered looking at it, but then putting it in her basket was lost in a bit of a fog. *Bugger it.* She decided they'd have to do without.

Poking the potatoes with the point of the vegetable knife confirmed they were done. She searched for a sieve in the cupboards but couldn't find one. With the steamer in use, she couldn't use that, so she decided to use the saucepan lid to hold back the potatoes while she poured out the water. Moving to the sink, she began tipping. As the first bit of water slipped through the gap, steam caught her hand. She instantly swore and dropped the lid. The potatoes thudded into the sink all at once, hot water splashes speckled her hand, and steam rose into the air.

Overwhelmed by the slight burning sensation and the sight of the potatoes in the sink, Lisa felt instantly cross – at the potatoes, at herself, and the fact her perfect plan had gone wrong. As tears pricked at her eyes, she saw the potato masher on the side and threw it into the sink. With her attention elsewhere, the edge of the chops had started to catch. She turned the heat off and threw the grill, complete with chops, onto the hob before slumping down onto the floor by a cupboard and crying.

Nathan appeared in the doorway, taking in the sight before him. His dark blond hair was wet and ruffled from the shower, his muscular torso was bare while stretch jersey boxer shorts complemented his physique. 'Wow, what happened?' He crouched down in front of Lisa, his eyes flicking round the kitchen. 'How long was I gone?'

Lisa sobbed, aware she had made it all so much worse than it needed to be, but she just couldn't help herself. She wanted it all to be perfect. She attempted to catch her breath while Nathan looked at her. The concern in his blue eyes made her feel a fool. He dealt with real disasters on a daily basis, yet here she was crying because steam had touched her hand and the potatoes had fallen into the sink.

'Lisa, what happened?'

'I'm sorry … I need to tell you something.'

'OK.' Nathan stilled, concern etched on his face.

Lisa could see doubt and fear in his eyes and felt guilty. 'It's not about us, it's me.'

His expression didn't change.

Lisa realised she was making matters worse. 'I love you. I just need … to talk to you.' She wiped her face and attempted to steady her breathing. 'Is that all right?'

Nathan held her hands and pulled her to her feet. 'Of course.' He looked at the food on the cooker and the potatoes in the sink. He switched off the steamer. 'Let's leave this. You go into the lounge. I'll put some clothes on and get us a drink.' He ventured a smile that wasn't reflected in his eyes. 'It will be OK, whatever it is. It will be OK.'

Lisa wondered if he was trying to reassure her or himself. She pulled him into a hug. Wrapped in the security of his arms, feeling the cool smooth touch of his skin and taking in the fresh scent of Nathan Baker after a shower, she wanted to kiss him, to forget about the disaster that was dinner, and the looming talk she knew they needed to have, but then what? Things needed to be said, and the time to do that was now.

As night had drawn in more fully, the candles cast shadows across the still features of his face. Without speaking, he leaned forward, rested his elbows on his thighs, and placed his chin on his clasped hands. His breathing was shallow. He had listened while Lisa spoke, not interrupting. Holding her hand and taking it all in. Lisa had seen the clench in his jaw and felt his grip tighten on her hand as she spoke about Ben. It wasn't easy saying how they had met. Not when she had left Nathan after his proposal at their prom because she didn't want to be in a relationship. She had wanted more, to see more and to do more – when she had met Ben travelling, carefree and embracing adventure, he had offered that.

When she told Nathan about the way Ben had treated her when they had returned to London, about his jealousy and how he hadn't wanted their baby – the baby she eventually lost – she saw the colour drain from his cheeks. She had managed to speak quietly, calmly about it. She wanted Nathan to know, but she wanted to protect him from the depth of the sorrow she had felt, too. Now she sat waiting, urging him to speak, missing the feel of his hand holding hers. She needed to know he still loved her, that everything would be all right, and that he didn't think less of her for staying with Ben longer than she should have.

She heard the tick of the kitchen clock and tried not to count each second that drew out the silence between them. Maybe Nathan would think she deserved the way Ben treated her. If she had stayed, not run away when they were teenagers, none of it would have happened. Why hadn't she thought of that until now?

Nathan let out a breath before looking at her.

She couldn't read his expression or the hard line of his normally soft lips.

'I am so sorry, Lisa.'

Oh no! Her heart thudded hard against her chest.

'I'm so sorry this has all happened to you. The baby.' He shook his head and rubbed his hand through his hair. 'You lost your baby and went through it all alone.'

Lisa sat, trying to interpret his words. She felt drained from sharing it all and scared of the consequences to their still-new relationship.

'I wish …' He stood and went to the window, staring out into the darkness.

She watched his reflection in the glass. When he turned, he offered a small smile. 'I wish I had been there for you. I let you go. If I had followed when you left, things might have been different.'

Lisa stood and went to him. 'But we're together now.' She tried not to reveal the question in her tone. 'I just needed you to know, not about Ben really, but about Pip. I wanted you to know about Pip.'

Nathan pulled her towards him as he sat on the window seat.

She welcomed his arms around her, taking strength from them.

Nathan sighed and pressed his forehead against her. 'I wanted to do all your firsts with you.'

Lisa ventured a smile, as she moved to look into his eyes. 'You did lots of my firsts with me.'

Nathan grinned. 'Yes, I did.' He kissed her before pulling back and exhaling. 'Can I be honest with you?'

'Of course. We need to be honest with each other. That's why I wanted you to know.' As she spoke she felt a tightening in her chest she tried to breathe away.

Nathan hesitated before speaking, 'I am so bloody angry right now, I don't really know what to do with myself.'

'At me?' Lisa's eyes searched his.

'At you? No! Of course not at you. I'd like to kill him for the way he's treated you, and I don't know what to do with that. I mean, if he'd treated you well, you wouldn't have come back and you wouldn't be here now. But the fact he was so ... so ...'

Lisa held Nathan's face, imploring him to look into her eyes. 'But I am here now, and that's in the past. Not Pip, the love I have for Pip stays with me. But Ben, he doesn't deserve our time. He doesn't deserve our emotions.'

'I know; I do get what you're saying. And I want you to know I am sorry you lost your baby.'

Lisa felt tears sting her already red-rimmed eyes. She had waited too long to hear Ben say that about his own baby, yet here was Nathan saying it to her as if the words came naturally to him. A sob escaped her and Nathan pulled her closer to him. She began to kiss him. Small kisses at first, followed by deeper hungry salt-tasting kisses that mingled with her tears. She felt how much she loved him as much as she felt the need to have him – a longing to connect with him. She shifted, straddling him on the window seat, and he returned her kisses, meeting her need. With Lisa's arms round his neck and her legs wrapped around him, Nathan stood and carried her to his bedroom.

Chapter Nine

Lisa was almost twenty minutes late by the time she reached the larger out-of-town soft play. The noise was intense and the atmosphere was a stark contrast to the bed she had left with Nathan lying naked in it. While he had slept, Lisa had got up, showered, removed the empty rocky road tub and spoons from the bedroom – that had answered their need for sustenance at two o'clock in the morning – and cleared away the mess in the kitchen. The note she left told Nathan to think of her at soft play (where she intended to have a coffee with Felicity and her friend Melissa while their children played) and that she would see him later after she had walked Jack and had a chat with Winnie. She also promised to bring takeaway back, to save any mishaps over food. Leaving Nathan to catch up on some sleep after he had recently worked two days, followed by two nights, prior to the night they had spent together, seemed only fair. He'd be off for another five days but she knew he intended to work on the renovations to the rest of the flats below his. Lisa wondered what it would be like once other tenants moved in; perhaps Sam's presence would seem less intrusive once there were others.

Melissa looked up and waved as she saw Lisa scanning the room for them. Lisa weaved her way to their table, dodging scattered shoes and empty chairs with jackets hanging on the back, as well as an array of parents attempting to make the most of their time while their children played – scrolling through phones, reading, chatting or generally staring into space.

'I guess the fact it's raining outside makes it super busy.'

Lisa took off her coat and placed it on the back of her chair before sitting down.

'Most days are busy at soft play.' Felicity grinned.

'What's the smell?' Lisa looked around.

Melissa picked up her daughter, Bella, and sniffed. 'Not Bella.'

Felicity looked around the room. 'I think it's just a wet coat and sweaty child combination.'

Lisa laughed. 'Ah, if it had been wet dog, I'd have got it. My van frequently smells of it. It's an occupational hazard.' Lisa held Bella's hand and chatted a greeting to her.

'She was playing in the baby area, but some bigger children ran through and put her off.' Melissa nodded her head in the direction of a table encircled by older children, who Lisa assumed must be the culprits.

'Bless her, I can see why that would be scary.'

With a voice that seemed an octave higher, Melissa began to address Lisa and Bella at the same time, 'So it's Mummy's lap and your Mr Snuggles now, isn't it?'

'I don't blame you.' Lisa looked at the soft play area: three floors of mayhem and madness as children ran in all directions, throwing themselves through squishy rollers, smashing into brightly coloured things she wanted to describe as punch bags, but that didn't seem right for a children's play area, and climbing up and whizzing down slides. There was a ball pit, but that seemed to be being used as a runway between two parts of the soft play. Looking up, Lisa glimpsed Callum and Fred. They both smiled and waved before telling her to watch. Making sure she was looking, Callum spun Fred while he hung on to something resembling a mini spinning door. Fred's little head whipped round and his blond hair stood out.

'Is he OK doing that?'

Flick glanced up at a giggling Fred. 'He'll be fine. He loves it here because they can all go in together.'

After enthusiastically watching three rounds of the spinning game, Lisa went on a coffee run. At the till she pondered buying each of the children a cookie, saw the price and decided against it. She loved Felicity's children, but four cookies equating to what she earned on an hour's dog walk seemed madness. She wondered how Felicity and Pete managed.

Walking back to the table with a tray containing three hot coffees, albeit in takeaway cups, felt precarious. She was glad to reach the table, sit down, hand out the drinks and pass on the responsibility for at least two of them.

'So what's been going on?'

'We're celebrating, aren't we, Flick?' Melissa looked at Felicity.

'Err, yes.' Felicity held Melissa's gaze and muttered something Lisa couldn't hear before continuing. 'I went out for a run this morning.'

'Yes, your run,' Melissa confirmed unnecessarily.

'That's great, but I thought you said Pete was working today.' Lisa held her coffee still as a crying toddler ran by.

'Yes, but Sue offered to have the children for me.'

'Wow, really? Pete's mum, Sue?'

'Yes, she's being nice to me at the moment and so I'm taking the opportunity to get a few extra runs in.'

'Really, that's great. So did you speak to her the way I suggested? Perhaps she realised she was being a cow.'

Melissa coughed.

'Something like that,' Felicity confirmed. 'Anyway, she had the children and I ran up and down the prom.'

'Wow! And how was it?' Lisa went to take a sip of her

coffee, felt the volcanic heat emanating from the sip hole, and put it back down.

'Better. I'm still not what you'd call good. But I am gradually getting better. Of course, I went quite early so I wouldn't see anyone I knew, and I was a massively sweaty mess in inappropriate running gear, but I did OK. I made it to the lighthouse and back, and I didn't think I was going to die. I had Robbie on my iPod, which helped, and I was out in the fresh air, and I was me for a moment, I was just me.'

'Sounds bloody brilliant.' Melissa smiled.

'That's great, Flick. I'm super proud of you.'

Felicity picked up her coffee. 'And you, how was your evening? Did your meal go as planned?'

Lisa smiled. She knew Felicity was asking if she had finally had her conversation with Nathan, but as Melissa didn't know about Pip, she was saving her further explanations.

'Not exactly.'

'Oh no.' Flick looked at her, frowning.

'That is, I buggered—' Lisa stopped, remembering where she was before continuing, '—I messed up the meal. Slightly burned my hand and slumped to the floor crying when the potatoes fell in the sink—'

'But—'

'But after that spectacularly embarrassing moment, I had a very good chat with Nathan.' Lisa met Felicity's gaze, confirming it was the chat she and Nathan needed to have. 'And then we couldn't keep our hands off each other. I mean, we had the most amazing, frenetic and then fabulous S-E-X,' she spelled the word out as if that made the conversation more appropriate for soft play, 'we have ever had. It was ...' Lisa paused.

All three women turned to stare at the man on the next

table, who had given up all pretence of scrolling through his phone to listen to Lisa's conversation.

Realising all eyes were now on him, he turned suitably red and looked away.

Felicity took a breath. 'Blimey, Lisa, I am so—'

'You're not pregnant, are you?' Melissa blurted the words without preamble or explanation.

Lisa sat back, stunned, and Felicity jumped in.

'Don't be silly. For one thing, Lisa would know that, and for another she and Nathan haven't been back together long; give them time.'

Not realising her words might be insensitive, Melissa continued, 'I remember my moods being all over the place, and having the best S-E-X when I was first pregnant – mind-blowing.'

The man on the next table adjusted his position in his seat.

Felicity shook her head. 'Melissa, it's not really appropriate to talk about sex—'

'Mummy, I need a drink.'

'Oh Christ!' Felicity jumped at Callum's words.

Lisa sat still, stunned by Melissa's unknowing words, grateful for Callum's interruption.

Melissa grimaced and apologised to Flick while the man on the next table was clearly laughing at their expense.

Her cheeks red, Felicity flew into mummy mode. 'OK, Pumpkin.' She rummaged in an orange carrier bag by her feet and pulled out four bottles of water.

Fred appeared as if on cue, his hair wet with sweat, his cheeks glowing. Megan and Alice followed, looking slightly less sweaty but equally as rosy. The girls said hello to Lisa before picking up their drinks and gulping down water until their bottles contorted in protest. Once finished, the girls gasped for breath while their bottles popped back into shape.

'Can we have a cookie now, Mummy?' Megan wiped the back of her forearm over her brow.

'I'm hungry,' Alice added as if seconding the motion for cookies.

'Cookies!' Callum shouted.

Fred did what Lisa assumed must be his happy dance, until Felicity questioned if he needed his potty.

Feeling bad for having not just bought the cookies when she saw them, Lisa stood. 'I'll go and get them some.'

'No, don't worry. Look.' Felicity slid her hand back into her carrier bag and took out a bag of Smarties biscuits. 'These were a pound for five up the road. Slip them in these napkins and we'll pretend we got them here.' She winked.

Lisa laughed, relieved the distraction from the children meant the conversation had moved on, and glad she hadn't spent an hour's wages on cookies that would have been surplus to requirements. 'You're a fab mum, Flick, you think of everything.'

Flick smiled. 'Thanks.'

As she drove a panting Jack back to Winnie's house, Lisa thought about Melissa's words. They had stunned her at the time. She hadn't considered getting pregnant again, not in real terms. Yes, it was a prospect somewhere far off in the future, but not in the here and now. Pregnancy in the here and now was still about loss, about Pip and mourning what might have been.

With Melissa's words practically winding her and the appearance of the children, Lisa hadn't had the chance to point out that the notion was silly. She and Nathan were always careful, and while her periods were irregular, Lisa was pretty sure she would know if she was pregnant. With Pip she had gone off tea and coffee and been quite sick from early on. Lisa decided she would text Flick later and tell her that she realised poor Melissa didn't know.

Winnie shuffled her slippered feet across the kitchen, carrying the cup, saucer and teapot-laden tray. It was a sight Lisa had missed while Winnie had been away.

'I'm so pleased your trip went well and you had a lovely Christmas with your son.'

Having placed the tray on the table with a chink of teacups, Winnie sat down and wiggled her bottom to the back of the seat. 'And I've got you to thank for it, my lovely. I never would have gone and done it without your encouragement, but you—'

'I just reminded you of your own good advice, and you're the one who's always saying life's too short.'

Winnie reached over for the biscuit barrel and started pulling at the worn gold handle on the lid. 'It's too damn short to waste trying to get this lid off, that's for sure.'

Lisa laughed, tentatively offering to help. Winnie wasn't always a great accepter of help and Lisa didn't like to offend her.

'Well, my lovely, if we're to have biscuits this side of sunset, you might need to.' Winnie pushed the barrel across the G-Plan table towards Lisa.

Lisa popped the lid off and welcomed the sight of the custard creams she knew Winnie had got for her and the overwhelming smell of the ginger nuts ever present in the bottom of the barrel – Winnie's favourites – that she'd got used to tainting them. Winnie lifted the lid of the teapot and gave the tea a stir before shakily pouring them each a cup. Lisa couldn't help but think Winnie's hands looked a little more knotted and less agile than when she had seen her last.

'Well, my lovely, how was Jack? I hope he behaved for you, and that grandson of mine hasn't been spoiling him.'

Jack, who hadn't taken his usual spot under the table in favour of leaning against Lisa's chair, cocked his head at the sound of his name.

'He was actually a star.' Lisa realised she sounded a bit too surprised and adjusted her tone. 'I mean he trotted along next to me perfectly. Even in the woods he didn't try to ... I mean he seemed very content to walk by my side.'

'Ah, he's a good boy.' Winnie looked at Jack, her milky-edged eyes full of pride. She took a breath and picked up her teacup. 'Now what's this I hear about the pitter-patter of ...' Winnie paused to select a biscuit from the barrel.

Oh no. Not Winnie as well.

'Tiny paws,' Winnie continued as she dunked her biscuit in her tea.

'What?' Lisa's mind couldn't keep up. *Tiny paws?*

'Well, wasn't it a kitten going walkabout that got you in the paper?'

'Oh, that! Yes.' Lisa's cheeks flushed as she told Winnie about the rescue and how Harold Martin had seen her while checking on the squirrels. 'I thought squirrels hibernated in the winter, but it turns out they don't. They slow down, they sleep more, but they don't actually hibernate. Did you know that?'

'No, I never knew that.'

Ha! So I'm not the only one.

'But something I do know ...' Winnie took a sip of her tea before placing the cup back on the saucer decisively and looking at Lisa 'is ...'

'Yes?' Lisa leaned forward.

'In all my years ... I've never seen the bones of a dead cat in a tree.' With that, Winnie burst out laughing, wheezing from the effort and swinging her slippered feet as she tried to regain her composure. When she had finally steadied her breathing, taken out her laundered handkerchief, and wiped tears from her eyes, she looked at Lisa. 'You're a daft beggar, but we love you for it, don't we, Jack?'

And it seemed Winnie and Jack weren't the only ones who loved her for it. What she thought might turn out to be bad publicity was having the opposite effect. People were happy that Lisa was willing to go the extra mile, or fifteen feet up a tree as it were, for their pets when needed. Even Kaboodle's owner had been grateful, when Lisa had expected the woman to fire her for letting the kitten out. It turned out she had been struggling to keep the kittens in, with their pent-up energy, and that was Kaboodle's third escape of the week.

Lisa had had calls from several prospective clients off the back of the article in the paper and even had to turn down some dog-walking opportunities due to not being able to fit them in. As much as the money was welcome, she wanted to keep offering a personal service and one-to-one dog walks. It was what she felt was important and, though she wasn't about to admit it publicly, probably enough for her to handle. The visitors and followers to her Facebook page had increased dramatically too, though that might have had something to do with adding the photograph of Nathan holding Kaboodle to the page after her night out with Felicity.

Chapter Ten

Visiting the Chinese takeaway was always a pleasure, not just because Mr Chung served good food but because Lisa had grown very fond of him since befriending him upon her return to Littlehampton. He greeted her with a smile and a knowing look.

'Ah, Miss Lisa, you want usual for you and boyfriend, no?'

Lisa smiled. She liked the fact Mr Chung insisted on announcing the fact she had a boyfriend every time she went in. It was a stark contrast to when she had first moved home and would order chicken chow mein and fried rice for one and talk to him about her day because the alternative was to go straight home and spend yet another evening alone.

Mr Chung put the order through to the kitchen and then returned to beam at Lisa. 'You very happy now, Miss Lisa.'

'Yes, thank you. I am.' It was true, and while Nathan was a big part of that, she also knew her life had been enriched by Felicity and the new friends she had made over the previous months.

Mr Chung collected the white plastic bag containing several food cartons from the kitchen and placed it on the counter. As Lisa went to take it, he held on to it and leaned forward, looking into her eyes. 'When two people live under one skin – the heart beats strong, love grows and life blossoms ... I put in extra prawn crackers for you.'

Lisa had no idea what he was talking about, but she appreciated the extra prawn crackers.

'Have you been flirting with Mr Chung again?' Nathan looked in the takeaway bag and raised his eyebrows at Lisa.

'Who me? No. You know my friendship with Mr Chung is purely platonic.' Lisa reached up and took out two plates while Nathan got the cutlery.

'Really?'

'Yes. Although it could be verging on the mystic too, he got all weird on me this evening—'

'On you?'

'OK, at me. He looked into my eyes and said … well, I can't remember what he said, but it was nice, I think. About you and me.' Lisa followed Nathan into the living room.

Once the takeaway bag, plates and cutlery were assembled on the table, Lisa pulled her chair out and found Uno sitting on it. She picked him up, thanking him for keeping it warm, before placing him down on the floor. Disgruntled, Uno flicked his tail and headed for his usual spot on the window seat.

'Drinks, I forgot drinks.'

Nathan fetched two glasses of wine while Lisa took the cartons of food out of the plastic bag, along with the bonus bag of prawn crackers. Opening the lid to the chow mein, she gagged.

'You OK?'

'Yeah. It just smells really weird. Maybe it's off.' Lisa put a hand over her mouth and slid the carton towards Nathan.

'It looks all right.' He sniffed it before forking some into his mouth. 'It tastes fine. Maybe you've just had it too often.'

'I don't think it's that.'

Nathan ate another mouthful.

Lisa's stomach churned. 'Don't eat it if it's off; you'll be ill.'

'Honestly, it's fine. Here, try some.' Nathan lifted a forkful to Lisa's mouth, causing her to retch and run to the bathroom.

Nathan followed her and scooped back her long blonde hair with his hand, holding it loosely at the back of her neck while she heaved into the toilet.

'Go away. I'm being—' Lisa heaved again.

'Sick, I know, that's why I'm here.'

'But it's … gross.'

'Lisa, it's fine.'

'But … don't … look at me.'

'OK, I'll turn this way. Better?' Still holding her hair, Nathan turned towards the sink.

Lisa heaved again until she felt as if everything she had eaten for the last few days had been deposited and flushed away in the toilet. Eventually, she took the cold flannel Nathan had rinsed and wrung out for her and wiped her face.

Feeling a wreck, Lisa slunk back against the edge of the bath, wondering if things could get any more humiliating. Yesterday she'd been on the kitchen floor in tears, and today she was sitting wiped out on the bathroom floor, having thrown up several times – *in front of Nathan, for goodness' sake*.

'Last time I felt like this, overindulging in Dr. Oetker chocolate and Mum's cooking sherry was to blame. Maybe ice cream at two in the morning doesn't agree with me.'

'Did you feel OK the rest of today?' Nathan sat on the edge of the bath.

'Yeah, fine, a bit tired but—'

'I think we know the cause of that.'

Lisa managed to laugh. 'Why don't you go and eat. I'll get sorted and come back to see if I fancy anything, maybe some of those prawn crackers.'

'You sure?'

'Yes, go. I can't stop you eating every day, and if you don't go and eat the food, Uno will.'

Nathan shut the bathroom door.

Lisa stood up, looking at herself in the mirror. *Well, that was spectacularly embarrassing.* She scooped water from the tap and rinsed out her mouth before cleaning her teeth and rinsing again. The minty taste and cool water combined was refreshing – a definite improvement. Having bleached the toilet, Lisa put the lid down and sat on it, gathering herself together. She wanted to be sure the nauseous feeling had passed before attempting to return to the table. As she sat there, she thought about what Melissa had said. *Stop it, Lisa. Being emotional over one spoilt meal, having fabulous – OK, better than fabulous – sex, and being sick does not mean you are pregnant.* She and Nathan were always careful, weren't they? She thought about Mr Chung's odd behaviour and tried to recall what it was he had said to her. Gradually, the words began to come back to her until they sat, perfectly formed, in her mind:

'When two people live under one skin, the heart beats stronger, love grows and life is given.'

"Two people under one skin." Could it mean ...? No. Lisa knew she had to dismiss all thoughts of being pregnant. It was silly. She and Nathan had been careful since bonfire night. When they first got together after being reunited, the sex had been a rediscovery and an exploration of the people they had become in the eleven years they had been apart; it was amazing, unexpected and unprotected. But Lisa knew she had had a period soon after, and subsequently they had always been careful.

Nathan knocked on the door, asking if she was OK, causing her to jump from her thoughts.

'Yes. Fine. I'll be out in just a minute.' Lisa's heart began to thud a little too quickly as she thought about the fact she had been a bit forgetful lately – not closing the window when she was looking after the kittens, forgetting the apple sauce. *Is that new?* She looked back at the mirror. She had gained a little weight but nothing major. As her eyes met those of her reflection, Lisa realised she was letting her mind get carried away. It was ridiculous. Melissa should never have planted the seeds in her mind. But now they were there, she knew she wouldn't be able to just let them go. Pulling out her phone from her back pocket, she decided to text Felicity:

'Do you think I would know if I was pregnant?'

The reply was almost instant: 'OMG, are you?'

Lisa looked at the unhelpful reply and responded: 'I don't know. That's why I just asked you if you thought I'd know. With Pip I definitely knew.'

'Come round. Pete's out. I've got a test.'

Lisa looked at her phone, making sure she had read it properly. 'Why do you have a test?'

'Long story. Come round.'

'But I've bought takeaway I'm meant to be eating with Nathan.'

'You always eat takeaway. Make an excuse and come round. You want to know, don't you?'

Lisa stopped texting. Did she? Was she being foolish? She didn't even know if she could get pregnant after Pip, and then what if ... what if she were pregnant, but lost this baby too? Would it be better not to know? Her mind didn't have time to ponder that as her phone began to ring, and Felicity's name appeared on the screen. Lisa pressed to answer the call.

'Are you all right? Where are you?'

'In Nathan's bathroom,' she whispered.

'Right. Listen. Don't overthink anything. Just come round and we'll do the test and go from there. How does that sound? Or if you want to, you can do a test with Nathan—'

'No … no, sorry, I mean, I want to be sure first.' *Decision made.*

Felicity breathed. 'Nathan won't be like Ben. You know that, don't you?'

'Yes, I do. But I want to make sure my head really knows that. Does that make sense?'

'Of course, after all Ben put you through, it's understandable.'

'And I might not even be pregnant.'

'So we'll do the test and then you'll know.'

'Yes. OK.'

'I'm here for you, Lisa. Don't forget that.'

'I won't.' As anxious as she felt about the test, Lisa knew she was lucky to have Felicity back in her life; whatever the outcome, whatever Nathan's reaction, Lisa knew Flick would be there for her, the way she had been when they were children. But now they were adults, with grown-up problems to face.

About to hang up, a thought occurred to Lisa. 'Flick, isn't Sue at your house?'

'Oh bugger, yes! Come anyway. We'll hide upstairs.'

Chapter Eleven

Lisa pulled on to Felicity's driveway and the front door flew instantly open. Felicity met Lisa at her van, clearly attempting to contain a grin that didn't want to be contained.

Lisa shut the van door. 'I haven't got long. I told Nathan you'd locked yourself out in your underwear.'

'Wait. What? Why did you say I was in my underwear?'

'Because he offered to come for me, and I had to think of a reason why it had to be me who came to let you in.'

'But you don't have a key. Why don't you have a key? I'll get you one cut.'

'That's not the point. Nathan doesn't know that; have you seen my bunch of keys?'

They headed for the front door.

'Right. Right.' Felicity stopped. 'If I was in my underwear, how come I had my phone?'

'I don't know, Nathan didn't ask me. If he does, I'll say you were in the garden trying to get a better signal or something.'

'Good plan. Why couldn't Sue or the children let me in?'

'Flick, calm down, we're not trying to find an alibi for a murder. You told me to make an excuse to come over and I did.'

They continued towards the front door.

'Good point. OK. It's just, I'm excited for you and nervous.'

Lisa could tell Felicity was trying and failing to rein her excitement in.

'I mean, are you OK? Do you feel all right? I don't mean physically, but … oh, you know what I mean.'

Lisa looked at Felicity. 'I don't know how I feel. Let's just get the test done and see then.'

'Sure.'

Felicity led Lisa inside. She said a fleeting hello to Sue, who was sitting between Callum and Fred on the sofa. The boys had wet hair and were in their pyjamas, entranced by something on CBeebies. Upstairs Megan was reading on her bed while Alice was playing with her Barbies. Lisa said hello to them while Felicity told them Lisa was round to borrow some clothes and that they shouldn't come in the bedroom because she might be getting changed.

Alice looked at them sceptically. 'Won't your clothes be too big for Lisa, Mummy?'

'Cheeky!' Felicity put her hand to her mouth, causing Alice to giggle.

'I'm going out and I need room to eat a big dinner.' Lisa pulled at the waistband of her jeans.

Felicity looked at Lisa, her eyes wide.

As they pulled Alice's door to, Lisa whispered, 'Sorry. It's the first thing that popped into my head. I didn't mean—'

'Shut up, you daft cow. I'm not offended.'

'You're the second person to call me daft this week.'

'Hmm, might be something in that, then.' Felicity laughed as she led Lisa into her room and began rummaging in her drawer for the test.

Lisa sat on the bed. Now she was actually at Felicity's and about to do the test, she felt silly. Of course she wouldn't be pregnant. Like Melissa, she had been jumping to conclusions based on scant evidence. But she knew she wouldn't be able to move on and get it out of her mind unless she did the test. She fiddled with the edge of the duvet cover. 'You've finally got Alice playing something other than doctors. That's good.'

'Don't let appearances fool you. She's probably diagnosed all of those Barbies with something. Either that or she'll be amputating their limbs as soon as we go downstairs.' Felicity took the test out of the drawer.

Lisa attempted to push away thoughts of the last time she had seen a pregnancy test, when it had confirmed she was pregnant with her little Pip. The memory was still raw.

'Right, let's read this.' Felicity slunk on to the bed, next to Lisa, box and instructions in hand.

Lisa took the box and read the front. 'There should be two in here. Wait, are you?'

'No, I am officially not, and as of yesterday my period came.'

'So you thought you were. But Pete's—'

'Had a vasectomy, I know, but they can fail sometimes, and my period was late and I panicked.'

'Blimey, why didn't you say?'

'I didn't want to until I knew. I was basing it on a late period, Dr Google and the fact I was dizzy after a run. It wasn't exactly hard evidence.'

Hard evidence. Lisa thought about the case she was building in her own mind; that wasn't exactly hard evidence either.

'And … well … I was worried,' Felicity confessed.

'What were you worried about?'

'Hurting you, because of … well, hurting you, and—'

'Felicity Willis, you're my oldest friend—'

'She's back with the insults. I'm only four days older than you.'

'OK, you're the friend I've known the longest, and I'm lucky to have you back in my life. If something is going on with you, tell me. I want to know.'

'Sorry. It's just after you told me about Pip … and, well, it wasn't just that.'

'So what was it?'

Felicity put the instructions to the pregnancy test down and looked directly at Lisa. 'I was scared.'

'Scared? Why would you be scared? You're the best mum I know. How you manage with four—'

'But that's it, I manage four all day long. I manage the four of them, and sometimes ...'

Lisa put her arm round Flick's shoulder. 'Sometimes what?'

'It doesn't matter. I can't say it, especially not to you. You'll think I'm horrible. I am horrible.' Tears welled in Felicity's eyes. 'Sorry, this is meant to be about you. Let's do your test.'

'Flick, don't. Don't shut me out. Tell me. I won't think you're horrible. I'd never think that of you.'

Felicity wiped her face and took a breath. Lisa noticed her hands were shaking.

'Well, sometimes it feels too much. Sometimes I'm overwhelmed. Sometimes I want to only think about me. Isn't that horrible?' Tears rolled down Felicity's face.

Lisa walked into the en-suite and got a wad of toilet roll and handed it to her as she sat back down next to her. 'No. Not at all. I don't have children and I think it is perfectly reasonable to feel that way sometimes. When I looked after your four over New Year's Eve, I was bloody knackered. I have no idea how you do it every day.' Lisa sat back next to Felicity and offered a small smile. 'You obviously love them to bits; nobody will think badly of you for taking some time for yourself.'

'When I thought there might be another ... well, I thought ... I felt like ... do you remember at secondary school when we had that glass of water ...'

Lisa had no idea what Felicity was talking about now, but stayed quiet to let her speak.

'We kept adding spoonfuls of salt.'

Lisa nodded, vaguely remembering that.

'We kept adding more and more, watching it dissolve until it wouldn't dissolve any more.'

'A saturated solution! That's what it was.' Lisa smiled, pleased with the fact she had remembered. Generally during Mr Whitworth's lessons, she, Flick and Nathan sat at the back, near the jars of bloated pickled creatures, playing with the Bunsen burner taps. But they did join in when it was time to do experiments, so some things had obviously stuck.

'That's it, that's how I feel sometimes. I'm verging on being a saturated solution, and if more keeps being added, if more gets stirred into the pot, well, then I'll combust.'

Lisa couldn't help the giggle that escaped her. 'I think you're mixing your experiments there.'

'Oh, you get the bloody idea.' Felicity laughed despite the tears that rolled down her face. She wiped them away with the soggy tissue still bundled in her hand.

'Flick, you know you're a great mum, don't you? And you can take time for yourself. It's completely understandable.'

'I know. Thank you.' Felicity hugged Lisa, clearly grateful for her reassuring words. As she leaned back from their embrace, she picked up the pregnancy test. 'Now. Let's get you sorted.'

Lisa felt her stomach flip. 'It's probably going to be negative. I'm sure I'm being silly. We've been careful.'

'My recent research suggests only abstinence is one hundred per cent—'

'Ha! No. We certainly haven't been abstinent.'

Felicity laughed. 'Sure about that, are you?'

Lisa's cheeks flushed at how quickly she'd jumped in to say it.

Felicity grinned, raised her eyebrows and passed the test to Lisa. 'So let's do this.'

Having done the test, replaced the cap and left it on the side in the en-suite bathroom, Lisa joined Felicity back in the bedroom. While Felicity clock-watched, Lisa paced the room. She sat on the bed, looked at the pile of ironing, trying to determine whose clothes were whose, stood back up and looked out of the window.

'It's time.' Felicity gave her a smile. 'Why don't you go and look.'

'No. I can't. You.'

Felicity stood up. 'Sure?'

Lisa nodded her head. 'Sure.'

Felicity walked back into the room, holding the test. Her face unsure and her eyes brimming with tears once more. 'Congratulations, Lisa. It's positive.'

Lisa looked at her, stunned; she was pregnant. *PREGNANT!* The word rushed round her mind as she absorbed Felicity's congratulations. Nobody had congratulated her on being pregnant with Pip. To be fair she had only told Ben, but this time around, hearing 'congratulations' at the same moment as she learnt she was pregnant was overwhelming. She flopped on to the bed. 'I'm pregnant.' Happy sobs escaped her. 'It's Nathan's. I'm pregnant with Nathan Baker's baby.'

'The amount of times I thought you were going to tell me that when we were teenagers.' Felicity laughed as she joined Lisa with the release of happy tears.

Lisa giggled, releasing some of her earlier tension. 'Sorry to have kept you waiting.'

'I'm sure it will be worth the wait.' Felicity smiled.

Chapter Twelve

Lisa looked at her phone balanced on the edge of Doc McFluffins' hutch. She listened to Felicity laughing at her predicament through the speaker while she manoeuvred carefully round the rabbit to fill up his food bowls and hay rack.

'Seriously, Flick, it's not funny. One minute I was watching Nathan steadily breathing in his sleep, trying to settle my thoughts by reminding myself how lucky I was, and the next I woke up sweating, eyes wide, having dreamt I'd pickled my baby.'

'Lisa, don't worry. Lots of women drink wine, or worse, before they know they're pregnant.'

'But what if that's harmed the baby? I never would have drunk it if I'd known. I Googled it and—'

'Stay away from Google. Please. You'll worry yourself silly.'

Lisa thought back to her dream. 'The baby won't look all bloated, like one of those creatures we had in jars at the back of the science lab, will it, Flick?'

'No. Of course it won't. I think your mind is just on overdrive.'

Lisa heard the giggle in Flick's voice despite her attempting to mask it with a cough.

'I think you need to focus on telling Nathan.'

'I am going to, but I wanted to wait until now. I think telling him on Valentine's Day will make it really special. I probably should have done the test with him. Finding out together would have been better, but I think he'll like what I've got planned too.'

'Good, and then you can call the doctor's and find out about booking in with a midwife. There's no hurry, as it's probably early days, but all of these things will put your mind at rest.'

'Yes. You're right. I know you're right. I'll stay focused.' Lisa jumped as Doc McFluffins went to nip her hand. 'Oh my god, Flick, not only have I drunk wine, I've cleaned up cat poo and I've climbed a tree – a tree, for goodness' sake. What if I'd slipped or fallen? What if—'

'Honestly, you just need to relax. Start by telling Nathan, and, Lisa, I'm sure it will all be fine.'

As Lisa agreed, they said their goodbyes. *It will all be fine*, she reminded herself. But she wished she knew that for sure. Doc McFluffins twitched his nose at her, and his whiskers vibrated inquisitively. 'What do you think, Doc?'

The rabbit thumped his back legs and ran into the covered part of his hutch with a piece of cabbage leaf.

'Hmm, Flick's right. I need to speak to a real doctor, and let's hope he'll be more reassuring.'

Back at her parents' home, ready to put her Valentine's Day plan into action, Lisa looked at the picture of the pregnancy test on her phone and smiled at the word on the screen, *pregnant*. She took the picture because with Pip, she hadn't made it as far as the first scan; she had no evidence other than the memory of the too-brief time Pip had lived inside her to show for her baby's being. This time around she wanted a keepsake and had insisted on taking the picture before Felicity disposed of the test. While Flick had mentioned leaving it around to give Sue something to think about, Lisa had managed to convince her that keeping Sue on side so she would continue to have the children occasionally, enabling Flick to have a little free time and to go for a run, was probably smarter.

With it being her first Valentine's Day with Nathan since they had got back together, Lisa had spent a long time considering what to do, and what to get him. As they were both working from early in the morning, they had decided not to see each other until the evening; Nathan suggested that they go to Cin Cin. Lisa would have preferred somewhere more private for what she had planned but didn't want to spoil the surprise by saying so. Instead, she used Pete's connections with the owners to secure them a round table. That way, they would have a degree of privacy and wouldn't be sat at one of the long, copper-topped communal tables. She had also called in earlier in the day to speak to the owner to check everything was ready and there would be no hiccups to her plan. *A special meal take three!* Tonight there would be no potatoes-in-the-sink disaster or issues with the smell of the food – she had checked the menu and carefully considered what to eat. She was ready. Well, technically she still needed to shower, do her hair and make-up, and get dressed, but mentally she was ready.

Finally, Lisa looked in the mirror and smiled. It made a change to get dressed up as opposed to being in her work clothes or jeans and casual T-shirt. The glacial blue material of her dress matched her eyes, while the delicate floral detail added a splash of colour. She liked the no-sleeves, halter-neck style. The dress accentuated her fuller-than-usual bust, before falling to mid-thigh. She had scooped her hair into a loose chignon bun, and slipped on her linen-blend cardigan and shoes. Now, she was truly ready.

When the doorbell rang, Lisa took a steadying breath before answering it. Taking in the sight of Nathan on her parents' doorstep made her pleased she had made an effort and sorry they had planned to go out. His charcoal grey fitted suit revealed broad shoulders and honed muscles, his classic white shirt was open at the neck, and she tried to focus enough not to think about pulling him closer and unbuttoning the rest of it.

Nathan paused, looking at her – a glint in his deep blue eyes and the hint of a wicked smile. 'Wow! You look amazing.'

Lisa smiled, and her cheeks flushed. It was good to know she was having a similar effect on him.

'Happy Valentine's Day, shall we go?'

'Yes … happy Valentine's Day.' Nathan leaned in and kissed her.

He smelt every bit as good as he looked.

Slipping on her coat and closing the door behind her, Lisa welcomed the cool evening air to calm her nerves and her desire.

Cin Cin was as busy as Lisa thought it would be on Valentine's night, but with nearly all of those there being couples out for an evening meal, the general noise level meant the two of them could speak easily. Lisa ordered water with the offer to drive home, while Nathan ordered a Peroni. The table was intimate and lit by a tea light in a glass lantern. The flame flickered as they took their seats.

Lisa placed her hand on Nathan's thigh, feeling his muscle flex at her touch through the smooth fabric of his trousers. She thought about the surprise waiting for him out the back of the restaurant, and reminded herself to breathe – slowly, steadily. If ever she needed to channel Dom's superpower for staying calm, it was now. She knew telling Nathan, sharing the news that she was expecting his baby, would be oh so very different to when she had told Ben she was pregnant. That was why she wanted to do it differently.

Despite her own fears about being pregnant again, she wanted to experience sharing the news in a happy, romantic way. The baby growing inside her deserved that; no matter what lay ahead, she wanted that moment for the baby, for her and for Nathan. Unlike Ben, who never wanted to share her with a baby, she knew Nathan wanted a family. They had spoken about it. Of course, that was before he knew about Pip, and they had been talking about the future, but she was sure, at least she hoped, the timing wouldn't matter. *Everything will be fine.*

Looking at Lisa with the hint of a nervous smile, Nathan placed a white gift bag she hadn't seen him bring in to the restaurant, on the table in front of her. Touched by the lovely surprise, before realising she hadn't got a gift to give him at the start of the meal, she bit her lip. She had thought so much about everything else she hadn't thought of that.

Nathan shifted in his seat. 'I hope you like it.'

Aware that her hesitation was adding to his nerves, Lisa slid her hand into the bag, taking out a flat white box, with a ribbon tied in a bow across one corner. She recognised the name of the jewellers embossed on the top. With shaky hands she slipped the lid off, revealing a black satin interior, upon which lay a bracelet with a heart clasp and three charms she knew had been thoughtfully chosen for her. 'Wow! Nathan, thank you,' she breathed. Removing the bracelet carefully from the box, she laid it in her hand, smiling as she looked more closely at each of the charms. It felt cool against her skin. It was so very different to the gifts Ben had bought her when they lived in London; they were expensive, impersonal, selected for show not sentiment. The bracelet Nathan had chosen, along with the charms he had placed on it, made her heart thud a little faster.

Nathan spoke, his voice unsure. 'It's white gold. I didn't know if you'd prefer silver or gold.'

'It's beautiful.' Lisa felt a lump forming in her throat.

'I thought about getting you other sorts of jewellery ... like earrings, a necklace ...'

Lisa looked at the flush spreading on his cheeks, aware that he was trying to avoid the engagement ring insinuation, and felt guilty that her reaction over eleven years ago had caused him to feel wary about the subject, even now.

He continued, 'And then I saw this and thought ... I thought we could fill it with memories.'

'Nathan, it's perfect.' Lisa felt tears well in her eyes as she held the first of the charms between her fingers. It was a satchel engraved with a date.

'I'm not sure about that one. I know it wasn't actually a satchel, and I didn't know if you'd remember.'

'The year we first started going out together, or the fact you used to carry my school bag?'

Nathan smiled, relief evident in his eyes. 'But I guess you do.'

'Of course I do.' Lisa looked at the other two charms.

Nathan cleared his throat and shifted in his seat. 'Right up until your recent escapade, those two made complete sense. Now I feel the need to point out they have nothing to do with you being stuck in a tree.'

Lisa laughed. 'In that case the firefighter is you, and the cat is Uno.'

'Yes! I'd ordered them before your daring deed.'

Lisa thought about the risk she had unwittingly taken climbing the tree and tried not to let her smile fade.

'Anyway, strictly speaking, the firefighter is from me, and the cat is from Uno. He asked me to give it to you since you've stolen his heart … I hope the bracelet's OK? I can change it if you'd rather have something else.'

Lisa draped the bracelet over her wrist and took a breath while she steadied her emotions. 'It's perfect. Will you help me?' She held her wrist up to Nathan.

He closed the clasp before holding her wrist and tracing his thumb around the bracelet as it glinted in the light of the tea light. Meeting her gaze, he smiled. 'Happy Valentine's Day, Lisa.'

She leaned over, her hand sliding along the line of his jaw and into his hair as she kissed him. 'Happy Valentine's Day.' As she sat back, she knew that this was the point at which she should mention her present for him. But she couldn't. Instead she took a swig of her water while searching for something to say, and then it came to her. A distraction. 'I much prefer my present to Flick's. Pete's getting her running shoes, but he's booked her in for a foot analysis or something first.'

'A gait analysis, really?' Nathan picked up his Peroni and took a drink before placing it back on the table. 'That's great. So she's keeping the running up, then?'

'Yes, she's really enjoying it.'

'Good for her, and Pete for the present choice.'

Lisa screwed up her nose.

'Ha, well, it might not sound great to you, but a good gait analysis before you buy running shoes can prevent injury.'

'Hmm, I suppose that's quite sweet of him really, then. Flick has put her name down for the Easter 5K and so she was really excited about the whole thing … but I'd rather have my bracelet.'

As the waitress appeared to take their order, Lisa welcomed the distraction of looking at the menu. Talking about their food choices at least enabled the conversation to move on from Valentine's gifts.

Lisa tried to stay focused throughout the meal despite the building butterflies in her stomach making it difficult for her to enjoy her chicken with porcini mushroom risotto. She caught the eye of the owner of the bar several times, who had nodded to confirm that everything was ready, but still Lisa knew, no matter how prepared she was, she didn't know what Nathan's reaction would be. That was the unknown quotient. She hoped she had done the right thing. That telling Nathan while out was the right thing to do. Nerves began to bite at her earlier confidence. Maybe she should have waited until later, until they were back home, just the two of them. Made it more personal, more private. Maybe she should have told him before now. The moment she knew.

Lisa fiddled with the charms on her bracelet – her lovely, wonderfully apt Valentine's bracelet, which she and Nathan were going to fill with memories. The thought warmed her. His gift was so perfect, she wondered if what she had prepared was enough. Excusing herself, she decided to go to the toilet and to text Felicity. If only she had run the plan past her before. She could tell her what Nathan had got for her and ask for her advice. She and Pete had been together for years; Lisa was sure she must know about these things. *Trainers, Lisa, Felicity was excited to get trainers!* Perhaps Dom would be the better choice.

Lisa stood, but as she did so, she saw two waitresses coming towards their table, one carrying the box. Ordering Nathan a rocky road cake was easy, deciding she wanted one from Choccywoccydoodah in Brighton made it slightly more complicated and had meant a journey over to collect it before her final clients of the day. But the notion had been fuelled by memories of the two of them looking in the window of the shop at the elaborate cake designs when they used to go to Brighton as teenagers. While most things in the shop were beyond their budget back then, they sometimes bought sale items or smaller chocolates to share on the train journey back home. Lisa hoped he would remember.

As the waitress neared the table, Nathan looked round.

'Dessert.' The women – both dressed in black tights, knee-length skirts, black shirts and green ties – smiled.

'But we haven't ordered.' Nathan looked confused.

Lisa smiled and tried to keep her voice even, despite the fact her butterflies had gone into a frenzied flight in the pit of her stomach. 'We'll take it, thank you.' Her heart was thumping and she could hear the rush of blood in her ears. Lisa took a breath.

The first waitress placed the red cardboard box tied with a black ribbon down in front of them while the second laid down plates, forks and a knife before they both smiled knowingly at Lisa and excused themselves.

Nathan looked at Lisa, a slight grin tugging at his lips. 'What's this?'

'Your Valentine's gift. You've got to open it.'

'Is something going to jump out at me?'

'No. Open it.'

'Will I like it?'

'I hope so.' *I really hope so.* Lisa watched nervously while Nathan pulled at the ribbon. People at the nearest table were glancing over, and Lisa hoped they would soon lose interest so she and Nathan could share their moment with a degree of privacy. As he opened the box, an intensely sweet and chocolatey aroma filled the air. Lisa's mouth watered at the smell and the sight of the honeycomb, fudge, nougat, coconut ice, jellybeans and marshmallows encrusted in milk chocolate forming the rocky road nest on which two handcrafted white-chocolate lovebirds sat.

Nathan's eyes went wide. 'Wow! This looks amazing.'

Lisa realised without the note, the lovebirds might appear too much. 'It's from Choccywoccydoodah.'

Nathan looked at her, his smile revealing his recognition. 'It's great, thank you. And we'll finally get to share an actual cake, because you'll have to help me eat it. You know I have to pass an annual medical test, right?' The laughter was evident in his voice.

'That's my plan.' Lisa smiled, not wanting to give away the contents of the envelope inside.

Nathan looked at the cake a little longer.

Spot it, it's there, look! Lisa wished she had thought through the red envelope in the red box, in a candlelit room.

Nathan closed the lid. 'Do you want some here or back at mine?'

About to suggest Nathan look in the box again, Lisa thought about the two of them, back at his flat, away from the noise and busy atmosphere of Cin Cin, and knew that was the way it should be. Private. Personal. 'At yours.'

Uno met them as they walked through the door, purring round their legs and rubbing his sides against them as he flicked his tail. Lisa slipped off her shoes and crouched to speak to him. 'Thank you for the charm, Uno. It's gorgeous. You're one of my favourite valentines.' She rubbed the soft fur around his ears.

'I hope you mean he's your second-favourite valentine.' Nathan put the cake box on the table, removed his jacket and pulled Lisa towards him. 'I've been waiting to do this all night.' He wrapped her in his arms and kissed her.

Nathan's touch over the light fabric of her dress caused her breath to hitch and sent sensations through her body as she returned his kisses and welcomed the embrace. Lisa's hands reached round his back, feeling the dip of his spine and the flex of his muscles through the cotton of his shirt, before she began to tug it loose.

The early morning sunlight shone through the curtains of Nathan's bedroom, waking Lisa. She stretched and allowed her eyes to adjust before looking at her bracelet. *Perfect.* Moving her hand to Nathan's side of the bed, she realised it was still warm, but he wasn't there. She thought about the cake they'd left in the box on the table and sat up. She didn't want Nathan to discover the note alone. She wanted to be with him to gauge his reaction and, hopefully, share the happy moment. She stood, grabbing the sheet and wrapping it round herself, but as she did so, the bedroom door opened.

'I've made tea.' Nathan walked in, dressed in black boxer trunks and a white T-shirt, holding two mugs of freshly made tea. His hair was suitably ruffled after the night they had shared.

Watching him, Lisa sat back down on the bed. 'Thank you.' *He hasn't seen it.*

He walked to his side of the bed, put the tea down and joined her. 'And I thought we'd have breakfast in bed.' He leaned over, picked up two plates from the floor, and then lifted the cake box on to the mattress, placing it between them. 'Well, I guess it's technically dessert in bed, seeing as you distracted me from having dessert last night.'

Lisa laughed. 'I think you were the one doing the distracting. But I'd love some now.' She pushed her fingers through her hair and wiped her hands over her face.

Nathan went to open the box.

'Wait. Let me go to the loo and then I'll be back.' Lisa decided she needed to brush her hair, clean her teeth and wash her face. She wanted to remember this moment positively, not wishing she didn't have bed hair and morning breath.

'OK.' Nathan laughed.

Lisa picked up his discarded shirt, still on the bedroom floor from the night before, put it on and grabbed her underwear. About to leave the room, she turned and pointed at the box. 'Don't open that without me.'

'OK.' Nathan looked at her quizzically.

'I mean it. Please wait for me.'

Nathan raised an eyebrow. 'OK, I'll wait.'

'Promise?'

'Promise.' Nathan threw a pillow at her. 'Now go.'

Once back in the room, Lisa picked up the pillow and sat excitedly on the bed, placing the pillow in her lap. 'Right, I'm ready. Open it.'

Nathan laughed at her excitement and opened the box.

The smell was still delicious, sweet and rich. Nathan put his hands in to lift the cake and stopped, seeing the envelope for the first time. He looked at Lisa as he took it out.

'That was the rest of your gift.'

Eyes flicking between Lisa and the envelope, he opened it and slipped the note out.

Lisa watched nervously, attempting to gauge his reaction. Nathan's face paled; his features stilled as he read and then read again: 'Roses are red, violets are blue, now share with your girlfriend, she's eating for two.'

Lisa's mouth felt dry as she ventured a smile. 'I'm sorry I'm not a better poet.'

Nathan looked at her, his deep blue eyes unsure. 'Does it mean what I think it means?'

Lisa noticed the quiver in his voice. 'Yes.'

Tears welled in his eyes. 'Then it's the best poem I've ever read.'

'Really?' The word slipped out as a sob escaped her, and her eyes searched Nathan's expression.

'Lisa, I've wanted this for so long … you … the baby, to have it all at once … it's just so—' Overwhelmed by emotions, Nathan moved the cake box and scooped Lisa into his arms. 'Bloody brilliant. It's bloody brilliant.'

Lisa wept happy tears, wishing she could hold on to this moment. She was pregnant, pregnant again with all the hope and promise that brought. Nathan was holding her in his arms, and he was happy. It was perfect, scarily perfect. *Please don't let this end.*

Chapter Thirteen

'Oops, sorry, I could have told you the midwife would want a wee sample from you.' Flick looked at Lisa, the laughter evident in her eyes.

'Well, I couldn't go on command. It was embarrassing. Even the dogs I look after are better trained than I am.'

'What? They wee on command?'

'Yes, dogs are clever like that if they've been trained—'

'Well, this is not the conversation I was expecting at my last Jiggle and Sing before I go back to work.' Melissa leaned down to Bella, who was sitting between her feet, and refastened the hair slide that had slipped down the silky threads of her too-long fringe. Welcoming her mum's attention, Bella gave a dribbly grin, showing all of her five milk teeth, before returning her attention to attempting to reach Fred's Thomas the Tank Engine.

The official jiggle and sing part of the morning being over, Lisa, Felicity and Melissa were sitting with a cup of tea in hand while Bella and Fred played with an array of toys that reminded Lisa of the jumble-sale toys her Granny Blake used to get for her when she was a child. The day she realised her mum had been lying when she told her the toys always had to go back at bedtime was still ingrained in her memory. With the hindsight of adulthood she could see why the slightly grubby offerings weren't up to her mum's standards, but still the image of the bouncy hopper she had loved for a full six hours meeting an untimely end in the jaws of the dustcart stayed with her.

'Normally, it's the children's toilet habits that fill the conversation—'

'Especially since Fred's started potty-training,' Flick interjected.

Lisa grimaced. 'Sorry, it's just it's all so new to me—'

'Don't be silly,' Melissa reassured her. 'I was joking. Bella's not one yet; I remember how I felt when I went to my first appointment. I was terrified the pot of wee was going to come open in my bag on the way. I wrapped it up so much that when I got there, undoing it was like pass the parcel.'

Lisa laughed so as not to reveal the things she had been scared of – talking about her previous miscarriage, and the fact the midwife said they'd leave listening to the heartbeat until her next appointment, as it was probably too early to hear it.

'As it happened, the pot coming open in my bag would have been the least of my embarrassing pregnancy stories.'

'Oh no. Really? Why, what happened?' Lisa looked at Melissa, eyes wide.

Felicity bit her lip, clearly knowing how this story ended.

'Let's just say it involved—'

'Wait.' Felicity sat forward. 'Do you need the potty, Fred?'

'No, Mummy.'

'Then why are you dancing?'

Fred shrugged and Felicity sat back in her seat. 'OK.'

'It involved a family dinner at Adam's mum's, a baby sitting on my bladder, and the fact I had a cold.'

'Oh no.' Lisa sat anticipating the end of the story.

'Yep! I sneezed and—'

'Uh-oh, potty, Mummy.'

All eyes turned to Fred as he stood, a dark patch spreading on the front of his beige corduroy dungarees.

'Oh, Fred, you're supposed to tell Mummy before you do it.' Felicity tucked her tea out of the reach of little hands and picked up the potty concealed in a carrier bag under her chair and Fred's Thomas the Tank Engine rucksack before leading a slightly soggy Fred off to the baby change room.

Melissa nodded her head. 'And that's pretty much what happened. In the lounge. In front of Adam's parents! Can you imagine?'

Lisa shook her head, not wanting to imagine and hoping that never happened to her.

When Felicity returned, Fred was trundling along at her side, wearing a slightly too short pair of tracksuit bottoms. 'Note to self, remember to check the clothes in the spare bag are still in the size your child is wearing. Oops, look at him, poor love.'

'He could audition for *Oliver*.' Melissa laughed.

Flick picked up and threw a soft cube at Melissa. The bell inside jingled as it bounced off her. 'And there I was feeling sad this was your last Jiggle and Sing.'

'I know, me too. Back to work.' Melissa shuddered. 'I'm still trying to get my head round that.' She picked Bella up on to her lap. 'I'm choosing to remain in denial about this one starting nursery.'

'I'm sure you are. But you know it will be all right. Bella will be fine.' Felicity sat down, retaking her place in the circle of seats. 'She'll have a good time, meet new people, make friends, and remember, even if she cries when you drop her off, it won't be long before she'll be crying because you came to pick her up.'

Thinking about the things she had heard Felicity say she missed, Lisa added, 'And you'll be able to have adult conversation.'

'You do remember I'm a teacher, don't you? Adult conversation is limited.' Melissa laughed, returning a wriggling Bella to the floor and the toys she wanted to play with.

'Oh ... yes! Well, at least you'll get to dress up and go and do adult things,' Lisa corrected.

'I miss adult things.' Felicity sighed. 'But,' she picked Fred up and blew a raspberry into his neck, causing him to shriek with giggles before she stood him back down, 'I've realised something recently; while I definitely don't want more children, Fred is my last baby. I won't be doing any of it again. I won't be pregnant; I won't have a baby again.'

'But you're OK with that.'

'Yes, definitely, but I'm also aware that one day, before I know it, it will be the last day I pick Fred up and carry him – seriously, I can't pick Megan up now, and I can barely lift Alice, and I don't know when the last time I carried them anywhere was. Or when the last time I read the girls a bedtime story was. I don't know when reading time instead of story time became their new norm. It all slips by so quickly.'

Lisa and Melissa looked at Felicity as she continued.

'So while I know I need more me time – for my own sanity, I think that's important – I also have to make the most of this little monster while he's still my baby.' Felicity scooped Fred up again, causing him to shriek once more.

As she stood him back down, Fred shouted, 'Mummy, potty!'

Felicity flew into action, grabbing the potty bag and taking hold of Fred's hand. 'Even changing nappies stops one day before you know it,' she called over her shoulder.

Melissa sighed. 'That's why I'm going part-time. I love my job, but I want to have time with Bella too.' She gathered up their empty mugs and returned them to the serving hatch as the group leader put the tidy-time CD on.

The children set to throwing the toys into two large bags the group leader had placed in the middle. Bella, who had been distracted by the commotion of tidy time, hadn't noticed Melissa had moved until she spotted her returning across the circle. For the benefit of her mum, Bella squealed. Melissa scooped her into her arms and looked at Lisa. 'How about you? What will you do about work? Will you be the Purrfect Pet Sitter plus one?'

Lisa sat back. 'I haven't really thought about it.' There was so much else to consider, so much else to occupy her mind when she wouldn't let herself think that far ahead. Nathan had suggested she move in with him and had spoken about completing the renovations on his house as one property as opposed to flats. And while that would be amazing, and an easy way to get Sam out of the picture, Lisa knew she needed to give herself time to get her head round being pregnant, to know that everything was all right. Thinking about work hadn't been a priority. 'I really don't know. I'm very busy at the moment. I'm already getting booked up for Easter, and some people are booking as far ahead as the summer.' Daring to allow herself to think how far into her pregnancy she might be by then, Lisa continued, 'I'm not sure how I'll do it all. I'm starting to feel a bit exhausted by the end of the day as it is. And I'm not exactly heavily pregnant yet, am I?'

'I guess it's tough being self-employed when it comes to things like maternity leave.'

'Yes. I will be able to do my job with a baby, and that's lucky, but it would be nice to have a little time off and know that my business will be OK. Nathan's shifts mean he might be able to help a bit, but other than that, I'm not sure I can trust someone to just take over the reins.'

'Unless that someone is someone you can rely on.'

'Yes, who's trustworthy and doesn't mind not earning a fortune while working random hours. Now where can I find that person?'

'Here.' Felicity's voice came from behind them. 'What about me?'

Lisa and Melissa turned to look at her.

'You just said you can do your job with a baby, so why not let me and Fred help you? It will be great. We'll be great together, you know we will.' Felicity noticed that Lisa and Melissa were staring past her at Fred. In his efforts to join in with the final part of tidy time, he was swinging a cuddly toy cat by its tail en route to taking it to the toy bag. 'He would never do that with a real cat. He loves animals,' Felicity reassured them.

Chapter Fourteen

Having excitedly discussed at length with Felicity about joining forces on the pet-sitting front, Lisa sat at her laptop ready to write a post for her Facebook business page. She had FaceTimed her parents the night before and spoken to her dad, who always liked to give advice when it came to her business. By the end of the call Lisa felt sure she was doing the right thing. She hadn't mentioned the baby; instead she had focused on the fact that having Felicity on board would enable her to take on clients she might otherwise have to turn down. It was a version of the truth.

Writing the Facebook post would give her the opportunity to introduce Felicity to prospective clients as well as those who occasionally stopped by her page with a friendly comment about the services she had provided. About to start, an email notification popped up on her screen. Seeing it was from *Paws About Town* magazine surprised her. Her old employer hadn't been in touch since she left London. In fact, none of her old colleagues had been in touch to see how she was, or to wish her well on her move.

Intrigued, Lisa clicked on her inbox. She read the post twice. It seemed the features editor wanted her to get in touch about testing out some products while "on the job" and reviewing them for the magazine. Lisa sat back. It had been a while since she had written anything. After Pip she found she couldn't think clearly enough to put the words together in the right order. Everything had seemed too meaningless. But now ... could she? It would mean a little extra money, and working freelance meant she could just do it from home – or her mum's home, or Nathan's home if she made the move – with the baby. It seemed crazy to turn the opportunity down; in fact, she wondered why she hadn't thought of it before. *Because thinking of London was too painful; because nobody from the magazine bothered to even ask how you were.* She decided to push all negative thoughts aside. This was an opportunity she had to take, and she wasn't going to allow negative thoughts to cloud her mind on the day of her ultrasound scan.

Sitting in the waiting room, Lisa's leg wouldn't stop shaking. As the only outlet for the nerves she could feel building inside, it had gained a momentum of its own. She had forced down several plastic cups of too-cold water from the water cooler, as the midwife had advised her to have a full bladder, but still her mouth felt dry. She attempted to read the posters on the wall, but the words wouldn't sink in. All she could do was look at the women surrounding them, each at a different stage of pregnancy. She envied those with big round baby bellies, drawing near the end of their wait. Nathan placed his hand on her knee, causing her leg to still. She looked at him and attempted to smile, but her taut lips were unco-operative. She wanted to be calm; she didn't want her fears and worries to mar the moment, but the image of the empty dark void on the black-and-white screen from her previous scan was still vivid in her mind.

When Lisa's name was called, she jumped. Nathan held her hand. For a brief moment before they stood, he looked at her, his blue eyes meeting hers as he smiled, and she knew this time would be different. This time it was all going to be OK.

The room was functional, but the sonographer and the nurse who had shown them in were friendly. Lisa lay on the bed with her leggings pulled down to just below her stomach. Nathan sat on the chair next to her, his hand holding hers. Lisa could feel the slight tension in his grip. As she lay back, she noticed the roundness to her stomach. She hadn't allowed herself to think too much about the fact her jeans were feeling too tight or that her bust had increased enough for her to have cleavage for the first time in her life. Both things could have been caused by weight gain. Until the scan confirmed there was a healthy baby growing inside her, she wouldn't allow herself to believe it was the result of her pregnancy. Once a tissue was tucked into the top of her leggings, cold lubricating gel was squeezed onto her stomach. Lisa sucked in her breath.

Dimming the lights, the sonographer began pressing and sliding a handheld probe across her stomach. His face was unreadable as he stared at the screen, clicking the mouse and occasionally tapping his keyboard. The noise of the action and the zoom of the computer seemed too loud in the silent room. Lisa wanted to ask if everything was all right. Why wasn't he speaking? Was the baby there? Was everything OK? Lisa could feel the tension building inside. She needed to know. Letting out the breath she hadn't realised she was holding, she went to speak, but as she did so, the sonographer turned the monitor.

Lisa stared, tears forming in her eyes.

'And there's your baby.' The sonographer broke the silence.

Lisa let out a single sob and Nathan's hand squeezed hers. She took in the sight before her, the outline of her baby's head, its button nose silhouetted against the black background and the roundness of its cheeks. It lifted its chin. The glow of the white outline of its chest and ribs flicked on and off the screen as the sonographer moved the probe. Lisa saw its heart pounding speedily and dared to look away, a brief glance at Nathan, who was transfixed by the image before him. As the sonographer moved again, the baby jumped, causing its limbs to stretch. Tiny, fully formed hands and feet.

'And it seems we have a big one in here,' the man added.

Lisa thought about the wine she had drunk and her dream about her bloated baby. Preparing to confess the thought was forgotten as, with a flick of a switch, the room was filled by the sound of the baby's heartbeat, the rhythmic rush and thud pulsing in and out – strong and vital. Lisa stared at the screen – taking in the image of the baby growing inside her. Nathan kissed her hand.

Lisa missed the sound of the heartbeat as soon as the volume was turned off. There was something magical and comforting about it. The sonographer looked at them, his face earnest. 'Now, I'm just going to take some measurements.' He looked at the nurse at the end of the bed, who raised her eyebrows.

Lisa didn't know what they were communicating but decided not to worry; all she had to do was look at the screen and feel Nathan at her side to make her nerves slip away. Once again the click of the mouse became the only sound in the room. Lisa watched as the screen was paused and measurements were taken of the baby via a series of crosses and dotted lines. Each time the picture was unpaused, she saw the baby move. At times, if the baby wasn't co-operating, the probe was wiggled on her belly, encouraging the baby to change position. Lisa was bursting for the toilet, but she didn't want the scan to end. When finally the sonographer looked at them, he smiled.

'So this is your dating scan?'

'Yes.'

'And do you have an idea of your dates at all?'

'No, not really,' Lisa confirmed, feeling a bit foolish.

'Well, your baby is measuring at eighteen weeks.'

'Wha—' Lisa couldn't finish the word.

'Eighteen?' Nathan looked at the man questioningly.

The sonographer glanced at a chart. 'So that would make conception early—'

'November!' Lisa and Nathan spoke in unison. Lisa knew the night had been special; the fireworks, the bonfire, the intimate atmosphere for two once they had returned to Nathan's flat – and now it seemed it had been special in more ways than one.

'My chart says November sixth, but these things are just a guide. And that gives you a due date of July thirtieth.'

Lisa's mind was still trying to keep up. *Eighteen weeks pregnant. How could I have not known that?* 'But I'm sure I've had a period since then, and wouldn't I … wouldn't I know it if I am eighteen weeks pregnant?'

'You'd be surprised. Some people can make it to the birth and not know until the baby arrives.'

'But shouldn't I be feeling the baby move? I could see it moving on the screen; shouldn't I be able to feel that?'

'You will feel it soon. Some first-time,' the sonographer glanced at Lisa's notes before continuing, 'some mums don't feel movements until later on. No two pregnancies are the same.'

'But how will I know the baby is all right if I can't feel it?'

Nathan squeezed Lisa's hand.

The sonographer smiled. 'Your midwife will continue to check that everything is progressing as it should, and you'll feel him—'

'Him?' Lisa and Nathan spoke in unison.

The sonographer hesitated. 'Or her. Would you like to know the sex of your baby? This will effectively be your twenty-week scan. Unless we have reason to see you again.'

Lisa and Nathan looked at each other.

Nathan spoke first. 'Do you want to know?'

Lisa hadn't allowed herself to think so far ahead. With Pip she had always felt her baby was a girl, but she never got the chance to find out officially.

'Only, if you don't mind, I'd like to wait ... for the big day.' Nathan rubbed his thumb across the back of Lisa's hand.

Her heart swelling a little at the look of love and excitement in Nathan's eyes, Lisa nodded. 'Yes, let's wait. We've already had one surprise today.'

By the time the scan was over, Lisa didn't know if it was because her hands were shaking with the shock of being eighteen weeks pregnant or if it was because the wad of blue tissue she had been passed wasn't absorbent that she was making a terrible job of wiping the gel off her stomach. In the end she put the tissue in the bin and decided to just pull her leggings up. Her head was too full as she tried to process the last forty-five minutes to worry about the cold squelchy gel on her stomach dampening her clothes.

After they said thank you and left the room, Lisa and Nathan walked hand in hand along the corridors of the hospital, neither of them speaking. Once outside, Nathan took in a big breath and looked at Lisa.

'Eighteen weeks, can you believe that?'

Lisa put her hand to her stomach. 'No, it's the best news.' She smiled, a full beaming smile.

'And that means we're having a baby in—'

'Twenty-two weeks,' Lisa finished.

They looked at each other, eyes wide.

'Bloody hell! We have seriously got some planning to do.' Lisa giggled, releasing her earlier tension as happy tears escaped her.

Chapter Fifteen

Felicity rubbed her wet hair with a towel before beginning to brush out the knots. Lisa made her a tea and asked Fred if he'd like some milk. Too engrossed in playing with his soft toys and the vet kit Lisa had bought him – her not so subtle way to teach him about appropriate animal care – Fred declined.

'So, how was the run?' Lisa placed Flick's mug of tea down in front of her.

Now Felicity's cheeks were turning a paler shade of crimson, she was showered and out of her new running gear, Lisa wanted to hear how she was progressing.

'Not too bad. I'm preferring the spring weather and I am attempting to stick to a schedule I found online, to help me prepare for the Easter 5K. Thanks so much for watching Fred. I think with you, Sue and Pete helping me get out regularly, I should be ready.'

'If anyone can do it, you can!' Lisa paused. 'Obviously I would have put aside my dislike of running and put my name down too, to support you, but there's the small matter of—'

'Being twenty weeks pregnant, I know.' Felicity laughed.

'Oh, have I mentioned that?' Lisa rubbed her hand over her stomach.

Felicity threw the towel she had used for her hair in Lisa's direction. 'And you know I couldn't be happier for you. But if you're going to update me daily on your pregnancy progress, I may have to—'

'Fine, I'll stop the daily count, so long as I can still—'

'Phone me first thing in the morning to ask why your boobs have more veins than before, or text me in the middle of the night to check the brown line snaking up your stomach isn't caused by the baby trying to escape because you and Nathan—'

'Lalala, little ears!' Lisa put her hands over Fred's ears as her cheeks turned pink.

Fred squirmed free, putting his plastic stethoscope in his ears in protest.

'Of course you can. That's what friends are for.'

'Talking of friends, did you know Pete has been texting Nathan lately?' Lisa fetched herself a glass of water.

'No. Really?'

'Yes. I think it's nice. Nathan has his workmates and some friends from the surf school he runs in the summer, but him and Pete being friends would be great for us too, wouldn't it? I mean proper friends, not just getting on because we threw them together.'

'Yes. It will make things like our trip to France easier.' Felicity took Fred's stethoscope and put it on, listening to his teddy's heart and confirming he needed medicine before continuing. 'Talking of friends, I saw on Facebook Nathan's still in touch with Brett Austin.'

Lisa thought about the pictures she had seen of Nathan and Brett together when she had snooped on his Facebook page after her return to Littlehampton. They had been best friends at school and had obviously seen each other in the years since. 'Yes, but he hasn't mentioned him to me, so I guess they're not as close as they used to be.' With all that had happened since Lisa had been back with Nathan, it hadn't occurred to her to ask about Brett. She recalled the various sights and scenes of his pictures. 'I think he travels a lot; maybe he's away.'

'Ah, OK. So what has Pete been texting Nathan about?'

'He ...' Lisa realised Pete might not want Felicity to know he had been asking about fitness watches, as it might be for a surprise for her, 'he seems pleased for us about the baby.' Sitting down opposite Fred, she decided to steer the conversation in a different direction. 'Do you think Pete would have liked another baby?'

Felicity picked up a toy thermometer Fred had dropped. 'No, not really. Don't get me wrong; he would have been great if I'd been pregnant, I know that. But I think he was more interested in calling a baby Thor than the idea of actually having a baby.'

'Thor? Why?' Lisa spluttered, attempting to swallow the sip of water she had just taken.

Felicity laughed. 'Don't ask. How about you? Thought of any names yet?'

Lisa put her glass down, wishing she had thought to bring the blackcurrant squash Nathan had gone out to get her along with the Maltesers she had fancied, the night before. 'No. Not yet.'

'What about a bump name?'

'No, no bump name.'

'Each of mine had a bump name: Bump – a bit obvious that one; Jellybean – I had a craving; Pumpkin – choose wisely, it could stick.'

Lisa thought about Callum's mop of red hair and smiled. 'And Flump.'

'Flump?'

'I'd like to say because I had an addiction to the sweets, but really it was because my belly got more squishy and striped with each pregnancy.'

'Oh.' Lisa giggled.

'So … what's yours?'

'We don't have one.'

Felicity went to speak but Lisa continued, 'Pip remained Pip because that was the size she had grown to on my pregnancy app. For this baby I want to focus on the name he or she will have at birth.'

'That's understandable.' Felicity bit her lip.

Hoping she hadn't made her feel uncomfortable, Lisa changed the subject. 'Did I tell you I think it's a boy? The sonographer definitely referred to the baby as "him" during the scan.'

'Really? He dropped the sex bomb? Even though you said you didn't want to know?'

'Yes.'

'Wow!' Flick shook her head. 'But I guess it must be hard not to let it slip.'

'He added "or her" quite quickly after.'

'Hmm, so either it was a slip, or he said "him" because he was trying not to let you know it was a girl.'

'A girl?' Fred stopped what he was doing to screw up his nose and look at Lisa. 'I want a boy to play with.'

Lisa picked up one of Fred's teddies – a fluffy dog complete with collar and lead. 'Well, it might be. But I can't promise.' Lisa wrapped a bandage round the dog's leg. 'Oh no, vet Fred, can you fix him?'

'Maybe.' Fred took the dog. 'But I can't promise.'

Lisa laughed.

As Fred set to with his patient, Lisa thought how lucky her baby would be to have Fred and the rest of Felicity's children to grow up with. 'He's too cute!' She smiled and took another sip of her water before changing the subject. 'Shall we look at this week's client list, sort appointments and look at the goodies *Paws About Town* have sent?'

'They've arrived?'

'Yes, the parcel's in my van.'

'Wow, that was speedy. And you don't find it weird, your editor getting in touch after all this time?'

'At first. But it turns out the features editor, Jane, had been having some personal issues of her own.' Lisa mouthed 'divorce', as if Fred shouldn't hear the word.

'I guess you never know what other people are going through.' Felicity drank the last of her tea.

'True. Now it seems she's back on top of things, and curiosity got the better of her about me leaving. She looked me up and discovered my Purrfect Pet Sitter page. In her words it set her "cogs turning".'

'Great. If it means you can earn some extra money before the baby comes, it's a win-win.'

Registering the unsure tone in Felicity's voice, Lisa looked at her. 'I'll still need to keep my business going. I still need you with me.'

'Really?' Felicity smiled, relief evident in her eyes.

'Of course, I can't climb trees now I'm twenty weeks pregnant.'

'Ha, that was not in my contract.'

'Flick, you don't have a contract.'

'Exactly!'

After Felicity made herself another cup of tea and found a blackcurrant Fruit Shoot for Lisa, they compared diaries and scheduled in the week's appointments.

It had only been a couple of weeks, but Lisa was finding Felicity's support with her increasing workload a great help. She was turning down fewer new clients and, since Flick had started taking on some of her existing clients too, Lisa was feeling less tired by the end of the day. While she had taken Felicity to meet Winnie and Jack, Lisa was in no hurry to stop seeing her favourite clients, especially not since Dom had pointed out Jack's new obsession with her could be down to her pregnancy, and Winnie had started knitting for the baby – no easy task with her knotted hands.

Once the week ahead was planned, Felicity fetched the parcel sent from *Paws About Town* magazine from Lisa's van. Lisa had saved opening it until they were together, wanting Felicity to know she welcomed her opinion on any of the gadgets they were sent. With the box on the table in front of her, Lisa opened it and peered inside before pulling out a round object wrapped in bubble wrap and secured with tape.

'It's like Christmas,' Felicity joked.

'Christmas if you have to unwrap your presents, test them out and send them back with a five-hundred-word report on their functionality,' Lisa pointed out.

'Hmm, not quite like Christmas, then.'

Lisa pulled at the last of the tape, causing the object to clatter to the floor.

'It's a lead.' Felicity went to pick it up, but Lisa was already stooping beside it.

'An extending lead.' Lisa slipped her hand to the floor sideways to avoid bending over her increasingly firm baby belly. 'Look, it lights up.' She pressed a button, causing lights to flash on and off.

'Can I do it?' Fred was watching them keenly.

'Not now, you can have a turn in a minute if Lisa says it's all right,' Felicity affirmed before turning her attention back to the lead. 'What's the bit on top do?'

'I think' – Lisa lifted the flap – 'it holds poo bags—'

'Haha, you said poo! Lisa said poo, Mummy.' Fred looked at Felicity, a cheeky grin spreading across his face.

'She did, but it's OK to say poo bags, the way Lisa did,' Felicity responded, taking the lead from Lisa and discovering another compartment. 'Treats too, by the look of it. What else is in there?'

Lisa looked back at the bubble wrap, noticing the other

objects for the first time. She pulled them out. 'Attachments, maybe, for more leads?' She looked at Felicity.

Looking at the high-tech dog lead in her hand, complete with LED lights, handy compartments and extra lead attachments, Felicity nodded and blew out a breath. 'It's the ... Swiss army knife of dog leads!'

Lisa smiled, the headline for her report having just been handed to her in Felicity's comment.

As the kitchen door opened, Sue walked in.

Waving his stethoscope in the air, Fred cheered. 'Nanny, come and see what Lisa got me!'

Felicity smiled a welcome, but Lisa heard the brief sigh she let slip too.

'Mrs Willis, Sue, you are looking well ... today.' Lisa attempted a Sueism, hoping to give Felicity a giggle, but realised her words hadn't quite come out in the manner Felicity described Sue's quips. 'I mean, your hair looks lovely ... now you've ...' Lisa paused, she had nowhere to take the end of that sentence without seeming extremely rude. Her cheeks began to go red. 'I mean ...' *Oh, ground swallow me up now.*

Felicity began to laugh.

Sue stared at Lisa, waiting for her to finish her sentence.

'Oh, poo bags!'

All eyes turned to Fred, who was looking at them with big blue innocent eyes.

'I dropped my dog lead, too!' He tutted.

On the doorstep Felicity continued to laugh. 'That was the funniest thing I've witnessed for a long time.'

Lisa put her hands to her face in shame. 'Thank goodness for Fred.'

'Yes, thank goodness my son repeats things he shouldn't.' Felicity grinned.

'Bless him, he's adorable.' Lisa lowered her voice, 'Will Sue be staying with you much longer?'

'Just until Monday. Returning her home before Mother's Day seemed a bit mean. So like the good daughter-in-law I am, I offered for her to stay until after the weekend.'

'You're making the most of her looking after Fred while you run, aren't you?' Lisa raised an eyebrow.

Felicity winked.

Once in her van and on her way to take Toby the Newfoundland for his swimming lesson, Lisa thought about Mother's Day. She had told Felicity she would accompany her to her mum's grave in the morning while Pete and the children prepared a special Mother's Day breakfast. Having not known about Flick's mum's accident when it happened, Lisa still found it hard to accept that Mrs Forster, or Mrs F as she called her, was gone. The trip to the cemetery also meant Lisa could take flowers to her Granny Blake, as she had promised her dad she would when they last spoke on the phone.

Lisa knew it was going to be a day of high emotions; the nearer it drew, the more keenly aware she became that this would have been her first Mother's Day with Pip. Of course she was excited about her pregnancy and the fact that she would, all being well, have her baby to share her next Mother's Day with, but, with Pip on her mind too, she also felt guilty for those thoughts. Add to that the fact she and Nathan had invited his parents for an evening meal, at which they intended to break the baby news to them, and Lisa could already feel the nerves increasing inside. Lisa hadn't seen Nathan's parents since her return to Littlehampton. She had got on well with them as a teenager, but after the way she had treated Nathan – publicly rejecting his proposal and leaving him the night of their prom – would they be able to forgive her and move on from that? Would they accept that she was back in his life to stay?

115

Chapter Sixteen

Sitting in her van, having bought the daffodils she wanted for the table, and collected the parcel containing the gifts she and Nathan had decided to give their parents with the baby announcement, Lisa read her dad's text and sighed. She had tried to FaceTime her mum to wish her a happy Mother's Day, but she hadn't answered. Her dad's response to Lisa's subsequent text asking where her mum was, thanked Lisa for taking the flowers to her Granny Blake and confirmed her mum was at her art class.

Lisa loved the fact her parents were enjoying their retirement in France, but she missed them too, especially now that she was pregnant. Thinking of them returning home for six months from Easter made her smile; she was glad they would be around when the baby was born – even if that did mean sharing a house with them. She knew moving in with Nathan made sense, but with his flat being on the top floor and the rest of the house still being renovated, she reasoned that staying at her parents' house, at least for the time being, made sense. As she went to leave her van, Lisa paused; and there was the other reason she didn't want to move in to Nathan's place.

Sam ran across the road from Nathan's building towards the tennis courts opposite. *She looks like a bloody gazelle!* Lisa attempted to slink down in her seat but realised thanks to the proximity of her baby belly to the steering wheel, her slinking days were over. Breathing in wasn't an option; it did nothing to alter her size. Instead she sat very still, attempting to hold her breath as if that meant Sam wouldn't be able to see her. Lisa watched, waiting for Sam to disappear behind the line of fir trees. She didn't have the patience for polite conversation today, not when she had the impending meal with Nathan's parents to think about, and certainly not while she needed the toilet and had to make it to the top floor before she could go.

As Lisa watched, she realised that Sam was talking to someone. *Ah ha, she's distracted!* Lisa got out of the van; as she glanced round to check that Sam was still otherwise engaged, she realised she was talking to a boy. The same boy Lisa had seen at the door to Sam's flat. *So surely that has to be Alex, blimey! She really did have him young.* As Lisa stood watching, longer than she intended to, she realised there was something familiar about the boy. She couldn't quite work it out, but he reminded her of someone. She decided she should ask Nathan more about him next time the opportunity arose. As Sam turned and waved, Lisa felt her cheeks blaze red. Automatically, she went to lift her hand but realised neither Sam nor the boy were looking at her. Instead they were looking up, towards the top of the building. Not wanting to be seen by them, or Nathan if he was looking out waving back, Lisa hurried inside.

Seven o'clock was racing around all too quickly. Lisa had tried on all of the outfits she had brought with her before she settled on the dress she had worn for Valentine's Day. It still fitted loosely round her stomach, and with her bolero buttoned at the chest, she was able to hide some of her increasingly ample – for her – cleavage. She looked in the mirror. Although her stomach wasn't huge compared to some of those she had seen at her midwife's clinic, there was no doubt there was a bump there. Nevertheless, the outfit did a reasonable job of disguising it. She didn't want Nathan's parents to take one look at her and guess she was pregnant; that would spoil the surprise she and Nathan had planned for the announcement.

Undecided whether to do her hair the way she had on Valentine's Day too, Lisa tried lifting it and then let it go. Usually straight, it had recently gained a kink, which she could only assume was down to being pregnant. She found it, along with her brown nipples, the line down her stomach and her changing food preferences exciting, as they were all signs her pregnancy was progressing, but also completely bizarre. Hormones clearly had a lot to answer for.

'You look lovely.'

Lisa turned to see Nathan looking at her from the door.

As he walked towards her, Lisa noticed his hair was a little tidier than usual and his face shaved more closely; she missed the ruffled hair and stubble look.

'Arghh, seeing your hair like that and the fact you've shaved makes me more nervous.'

'Don't be. I was just making an effort.'

'What, and you don't usually make an effort for me?'

'But I know you like the rough look.'

Lisa kissed him and then felt his cheek. 'Hmm, smooth isn't bad either.'

Nathan stepped back and kissed her hand. 'Now, before anyone gets here, I've got something for you. That is, Flick and I have got you something. Really, it was her idea.'

Lisa went to speak, but Nathan continued, 'We know it being Mother's Day has been playing on your mind, and I want you to know, we ... I understand – probably not understand ...' Nathan rubbed his hand through his hair, creating his normal ruffled look as he did so.

Lisa smiled.

'That is, I get it ... kind of ... I think. Anyway. Oh bugger. I thought this might be weird, I'm sorry. Maybe Flick should have given it to you—'

'Nathan, stop, I'm sure whatever you've got will be lovely.'

Nathan went to the drawer and took out a white organza bag. As he turned, she could tell he was hesitant. 'If it's not OK, or not my place, then it's all right to say.'

Lisa took the gift and slid its contents onto her hand. She looked at the charm, small and precious against her palm. She bit her lip, attempting to stop it trembling.

'Sorry. Would you rather we hadn't? It's just Flick mentioned it and I thought ...'

Lisa's heart thudded. Nathan's words faded, and for a moment all she was conscious of was the object in her hand. She felt overwhelmed, not only by the beautiful gift but also by the fact Felicity and Nathan had got it for her. Her two best friends knowing how she felt about this day, even without her confiding in them. 'Nathan, it's beautiful. Thank you.' She wrapped her hand around the white gold pip and welcomed Nathan's hug. As he stepped back, Nathan took Lisa's wrist and attached the charm to her bracelet.

She spoke past the lump that had formed in her throat. 'Is that OK, Pip being on my bracelet? You said it was for our memories.'

Nathan placed it before the other charms. 'You said Pip would always be a part of you. I wanted you to know I understand that. We both have pasts, Lisa, things that affect who we are now.'

'Thank you.' Lisa's heart was still racing as tears slid down her face.

Nathan passed her a tissue and pulled her closer for another hug.

'I'll mess up your shirt.'

'I don't care.'

Nathan embraced her. Lisa felt a strange flutter, a bubbling, no, tumbling motion in her stomach.

Her tears stopped as she gasped. 'The baby! Did you feel it? I think it moved.'

'What? No.' Nathan stepped back, putting his hand to her stomach. Lisa slid it to where she felt the movement.

'There, do you feel it?'

'No ... wait, yes. Yes! Is that it?'

Lisa nodded.

'I can feel it.' Nathan grinned at her and then looked back down at his hand resting on her stomach.

Lisa tried to keep still, willing it to move again. 'I think it's stopped.'

A buzz at the door interrupted the moment.

Nathan kept his hand on her stomach, but looked towards the bedroom door. 'That will be my parents.'

'You should go and let them in.'

'I'll go down to the door, give you a bit more time.'

While Nathan went to let his parents in, Lisa sent a text to Felicity, thanking her for the amazing gift and saying that she would call her later. She couldn't wait to thank her properly or tell her that she had felt the baby move. But right now she had the more pressing matter of sorting out her tear-stained panda eyes before Nathan's parents made it up the stairs. As Lisa moved, the sight of the pip on her bracelet in the mirror meant she was fighting back more tears. When she felt ready, she headed out into the lounge, feeling a little nauseous. Uno raised his head to look at her before resting it back down on his paws. Lisa could hear voices in the hallway and went to see what was keeping everyone. As she leaned over the banister, she was surprised to hear Nathan's parents talking to Sam.

Lisa moved down a couple of stairs, trying to stay out of sight. Sam was laughing. The entire conversation sounded light, but also as if they were all familiar with each other. It wasn't chit-chat between strangers. Lisa felt a prick of jealousy and another wave of nausea. She heard them ask Alex how he was, confirming the boy was Sam's son. Nathan's dad said it had been too long since they had seen him. Lisa didn't know what to make of it all. She and Nathan barely spoke about Sam. She was there, of course, an entity in the building. But they'd had so much else going on, she wasn't a priority in their conversations. Listening to Nathan's family talk to her and her son so easily made Lisa wonder what their connection actually was. Not wanting to be caught or to feel like the outsider in this conversation, Lisa slipped back upstairs and went to sit with Uno. Stroking his soft fur gave her comfort. 'What's going on here, Uno? Do you know?'

'Lisa, how lovely to see you.'

Nathan's mum walked across the room, her perfume reaching Lisa before she did. Lisa tried not to inhale, unsure if the nauseous feeling of moments before might return with a vengeance. She hadn't actually been sick for a while. Winnie – who had repeatedly told Lisa how overjoyed she was to hear her pregnancy news – had prescribed ginger nut biscuits for when she couldn't face food. That helped, but smells could still turn her stomach.

'Mrs Baker—'

'Valerie, please. We've all met before.' Valerie held out her hands and embraced Lisa.

'Yes, of course.' Lisa leaned in, going for a kiss to Valerie's cheek as the older woman merely touched cheeks. *Oh, fail!*

'And Uno, the rescue cat.' Nathan's mum stroked Uno's head.

'It's amazing, isn't it, how Nathan saved him?' Lisa smiled, remembering that Valerie always enjoyed talking about Nathan's successes – sporting, academic, it didn't matter – her son was her pride and joy.

'Yes, of course, but I really meant how Uno saved Nathan.'

What? Lisa felt wrong-footed for the second time since the door had buzzed. She didn't know what Valerie was referring to. Thankfully she didn't have to respond, as, before she could speak, Nathan's dad was greeting her with a hug, and a kiss to each cheek. Lisa attempted to smile while her mind tried to catch up. Was there so much she didn't know about Nathan? They had been apart a long time. But she was carrying his baby; didn't she need to know everything? Trying to rein her emotions in, Lisa took coats and offered drinks, before they all settled in the lounge making conversation.

Eventually excusing herself to check on the food, Lisa went to the kitchen. The grand lasagne al forno was bubbling away in the oven, filling the flat with a delicious smell. She and Nathan had opted for a Cook Shop meal after Lisa had reasoned it was more refined than a takeaway or a ready meal, but safer than home cooking after her previous culinary disasters. Lisa knew it was too much for the four of them to eat, but Nathan had pointed out having plenty meant they only had to do a simple salad to accompany it; Lisa conceded it was a good plan.

Pouring herself a glass of squash, Lisa took a moment to breathe before going back to the lounge. Valerie was being polite and making chit-chat, but Lisa felt the slight reservation in her tone belied the "why did you reject my son's proposal at the prom?" and "why are you back?" questions so clearly on her mind. Nathan's dad was as friendly as he had ever been, asking Lisa about her business and seeming genuinely interested as she chatted about taking on new clients and bringing Felicity on board.

'Everything all right?'

Lisa turned, hearing Nathan's voice at the kitchen door.

'Yes, thank you.' She spoke in a hushed tone. 'I think

your mum might need time to accept I'm not going to hurt you again, but your dad—'

'Don't let them get to you.'

'I was going to say your dad's as lovely as ever. You know, you're a lot like him. I didn't see it before.' Lisa smiled.

'I'm not sure if I should take that as a compliment or not.'

Lisa giggled. As she pulled Nathan into her arms for the fortifying hug she needed, Lisa wanted to ask the questions on her mind – *why are your parents so familiar with Sam and Alex, and what did your mum mean about Uno rescuing you?* – but decided it wasn't the time. What if she didn't like the answers given? Tonight was about sharing their special news; that was all that mattered now, wasn't it?

The door buzzed.

Lisa stepped back. 'We're not expecting anyone else, are we?' She looked at Nathan.

'Why don't you see who it is, and I'll check on Mum and Dad?' Nathan took the wine from the fridge.

Lisa wondered at the smile he gave her, and went to the intercom. As she pressed to enquire who was there, it whistled and squeaked. 'Bloody thing.' Fixing the intercom system was one of the jobs intended for after the renovations were complete on the whole building. Lisa could hear voices responding to her but couldn't make out what was being said. She walked out into the hallway and down the stairs. Walking past Sam's door, she rolled her eyes and resisted the urge to stick out her tongue, knowing it would be just her luck to get caught.

The nearer she drew to the bottom of the stairs, the faster she went. She couldn't be completely sure through the stained-glass panels and with the evening light outside casting silhouettes, but she thought she recognised who it was. With a broad smile and fighting back tears, she opened the door.

Chapter Seventeen

'Mum! Dad! What are you doing here?'

'Lisa, darling, it is so good to see you.' Lisa's mum smiled a broad, happy smile, welcoming Lisa into a hug. 'But don't swear on the intercom; the whole street could hear you.'

Lisa hugged both of her parents tightly, before she stepped back, taking in the sight of them on Nathan's doorstep. 'When I called, Dad said you were at your art class. But ... and now you're here.' Remembering herself, Lisa hugged her mum again. 'Happy Mother's Day. Come in.' She stepped back from the door.

'Thank you. We've been driving for hours. I couldn't answer when you FaceTimed, it would have given the game away.'

'Game away? What do you mean?'

'Nathan called us.'

'He did?' Lisa couldn't believe it.

'Yes, he asked if we'd consider coming back a little early. He said he couldn't tell us why, but that the surprise would be worth it. Your dad thought there might be an announcement.' Lisa's mum did an excited grin and squeal combination Lisa wasn't sure she had ever seen before. 'So here we are.'

'Well, if there is, you've just spoilt it.' Lisa's dad looked at his wife, shaking his head.

Lisa giggled before giving her dad a hug. 'It's fine, Dad. I'm just so glad you're here.' Stepping back from the embrace she beamed at the sight of her parents – still trying to take in the fact they were there. 'Come upstairs. Nathan's parents are here, and I think your appearance might explain why we have enough lasagne to feed the entire street.'

As she urged her parents upstairs, a thought occurred to Lisa; she hadn't cleaned and prepared their house the way she had intended to before they returned from France. She had been staying in their home for almost six months, and she knew her mum was a stickler for cleanliness. With so much else filling her mind, she wasn't even sure what condition she had left the house in earlier in the day. 'Have you been home yet?'

'No, Nathan booked us into a hotel for tonight. We said there was no need, but he insisted, saying you'd want to make sure everything was ready for us first.'

God, I love that man! Lisa breathed.

To Lisa's relief her parents and Nathan's seemed to have plenty to talk about. There were no awkward silences and the meal passed pleasantly. Finally, as they made coffees, Lisa and Nathan prepared to share their announcement. Lisa handed out the wrapped books while Nathan asked them to wait and open them all at once.

Holding Nathan's hand, Lisa watched in anticipation as bows were pulled off and the tissue paper was removed. For a moment as each couple looked at their gift, confusion flickered across their faces, until at last realisation dawned.

Lisa's mum gasped. 'Really? Does it mean? Are you?'

Lisa nodded.

Her dad wiped the corner of his eye before standing up to shake Nathan's hand and pull Lisa into a hug. 'Congratulations both of you, I couldn't be happier.'

Still a little dumbfounded, Lisa's mum followed, clutching her Ladybird book of being a grandparent in her hand. She looked at Nathan's mum. 'You know what this means, Valerie?'

Nathan's parents looked at each other and at the book; as they flicked it open, they noticed the scan picture tucked inside. Valerie took it and held it out so she could see it more clearly before looking to her son for confirmation.

'A baby?'

'It certainly is.' Nathan beamed.

For a moment Lisa thought Valerie wasn't happy, but as tears sprang to her eyes, she leapt to hug her son wishing him congratulations. And then, much to Lisa's relief she hugged her too, asking when the baby was due.

'That's the other surprise.' Nathan cleared his throat. 'It's due on July thirtieth. It's already twenty w—'

'Almost twenty-one weeks,' Lisa finished.

Lisa's Mum looked at her, shocked. 'Why didn't you tell us?'

Lisa and Nathan laughed before Nathan answered. 'We've only known a couple of weeks ourselves. We were surprised too.'

Nathan's dad topped up their glasses and proposed a toast to, ' New beginnings and the baby.'

They all raised their glasses. Lisa chinked her water glass against Nathan's wine glass and smiled, feeling happier and more relieved than she had for days.

'I can't quite believe it, and to think your father thought we were travelling back for a proposal.' Lisa's mum blurted the words, and the room fell silent.

Lisa felt her bubble of happiness pop as she looked at Nathan's Mum's crestfallen face.

Nathan squeezed Lisa's hand before breaking the silence. 'Tonight is about sharing our happy, baby news. That's what's important right now, but don't worry, when I propose to Lisa, we'll make sure you're the first to know.' Nathan raised his glass, said, 'Cheers, everyone,' and drank.

They all lifted their glasses and drank. As Lisa looked at Nathan, he winked.

When! He said when. Lisa, who hadn't dared to let herself think Nathan would propose to her again after her youthful declarations against marriage, held on to the word. Her head felt light; her bubble of happiness was well and truly restored.

Chapter Eighteen

Felicity's early morning preparations were streamlined by the fact she had remembered to gather her race number and other essentials together along with her running gear the night before. Aware that Ready Brek probably wasn't the type of porridge she should eat before a race, she decided upon a banana chopped in a little natural yoghurt. She took the folic acid and iron supplements the doctor had prescribed – not because she was pregnant but because her lack of essential vitamins and minerals had caused her dizzy spells. Felicity didn't know if her breakfast would be enough to keep her going and slipped a small bag of Haribo sweets, from the children's stash, into her bumbag. *That should help!*

Taking Pete up on his offer to sort the children so that she could go and get parked early at the seafront and establish where the toilets and start and finish lines were, Felicity gave each of the children a hug. Leaving the house, when there were four children to say goodbye to, always took longer than she anticipated, as each inevitably had pressing matters to discuss with her before she went. Rather aptly Alice was sharing the fact she was thinking about a new word, *nervous-ited* – meaning excited but also nervous – which Felicity confirmed was exactly how she was feeling about the race.

While Callum's mind was full of less apt but more ponderous issues: 'Mummy, when a baby is born, does some air get pushed out into space to make room for it?'

Felicity's mind boggled as she looked at him, dumbfounded.

'Right, shall we let Mummy go so that she can get sorted?'

Felicity welcomed Pete's interruption and managed to get to the door before being drawn into the complexities of Callum's question.

Pete hugged her. 'Stay calm. Good luck, and we'll see you there soon.'

'And you won't forget to pick up Lisa?'

'Are you kidding? I'm planning on her keeping this lot in check while I watch my wife strut her stuff.'

'I'm pretty sure there'll be more wobbling than strutting, but—'

'I don't mind watching that either!' Pete laughed.

Once alone in her car, Felicity felt a pang of nerves. *You can do this. You're leaving the house, and by the time you come back, you'll have successfully run your first 5K.* She glanced at herself in the rear-view mirror, hoping the resolve in her eyes would buoy her confidence. Instead, she noticed the dark shadows caused by being unable to get to sleep until one in the morning. *Oh bugger!* Deciding she was no longer nervous-ited, she headed towards the beach, playing with Alice's new word in her mind: *Petri-nervous, doomed-ervous, nervous-itting myself!*

Having parked her car in an overflow car park on the green, Felicity got out to hear music drifting in and out as it was carried by the breeze. The seafront was busy. People were swarming in different directions, some warming up, some milling around, most wearing an array of brightly coloured running gear and donning a race number. It was clear that along with the sun, more competitors than she had imagined and a good-sized crowd had come out for the Easter 5K. Felicity spotted the flags demarcating the start and finish line straight away. She got signed in and then set off in search of the toilet.

Standing behind many much fitter-looking, honed runners, gremlins of doubt began creeping in to her mind and playing havoc with her confidence. Checking the time on the Garmin GPS running watch Pete and the children had surprised her with on Mother's Day, she was beginning to feel a fraud. *What was I thinking? I can't do this!* The contents of her stomach flipped, causing a loud groan, and she danced on the spot, willing the queue to move faster.

'There's never enough loos at these things!'

Felicity turned to the woman who was speaking to her and smiled, feeling too nervous to make chit-chat.

Assessing Felicity's face, the woman patted her arm. 'Is it your first time?'

Felicity nodded, wishing her stomach would stop churning.

'I've only been running a year myself.'

A year! Felicity couldn't help but think that that seemed oh so much longer than her almost three months of attempting to run.

'Before I did my first 5K, I volunteered to help at a couple of local events. You get to see what goes on then and discover what's what.'

Why didn't I think of that? 'Wow, that's really sensible. I wish I had.'

'You'll be fine. Just remember when you go to line up, look for those who look like you. They'll be the newbies too. That's who you want to be with, so you don't get in anyone's way or get swept up into a pace you can't keep at the off.'

Felicity had no idea what the woman's words suggested about her appearance and didn't like to ask; instead she looked gratefully at the toilet door being held open for her as the runner in front saved her the 20p entrance fee and further wise words from the lady behind her.

Having calmed her stomach, if not her nerves, Felicity decided to head for the starting line and hoped she would see Pete, Lisa and the children if not en route, then during the race. She wished they had told her where they were going to stand so that she could look out for them. She thought again about the woman's words as she joined the procession of runners. *Blooming cheek!* But as she passed those with highly toned muscles and tanned limbs and moved further along those preparing for the race, she began to realise what the woman had meant. Felicity knew she had no hope of keeping up with some of these people. Spotting bunny outfits in three different shades of pink towards the back of the crowd, she knew she had found her own kind. The fun-runners, the sponsored-for-charity one-off-ers, and those carrying a what-have-I-signed-up-for expression – in short, the newbies. She slipped in amongst them and waited.

Hearing the final calls for everyone to line up and get ready, Felicity couldn't help but smile. She couldn't believe she was actually doing it. Her first 5K. As the starting pistol fired, it was some time before everyone had moved through the line. Seeing the number of spectators made her cheeks flare red. She focused on the sound of her breathing and her resolve not to trip over her own feet and land in a heap in front of everyone. Spotting some familiar faces and some amazing homemade banners in the crowd made her smile.

'Go, Flick!'

'Go, Mummy, go, Mummy!'

With Pete and Lisa's faces beaming with pride and the children looking so excited, Felicity knew giving up wasn't an option. *You can do this! Breathe deeply and visualise yourself running through that first 1K banner.*

Twenty-five minutes later and the lead runners, all seasoned athletes with tans that reflected their penchant for being outside, had already sprinted through, making it look all too easy. Lisa remembered her run along the promenade and knew it was anything but. As the time continued to tick by, the children were losing interest in everyone going past who wasn't their mummy.

'Do you think she's all right?' Megan was getting concerned.

'You know she was hoping to be under forty-five minutes. There's still plenty of time for her to make it through before then,' Pete reassured her.

Lisa looked at Callum, who was staring at her stomach. 'Are you OK, Callum?'

'Yes, I just wondered, when a baby is born, does some air … no, wait … how did the baby get in your tummy?'

Pete sniggered.

Megan looked at Lisa, eyes wide.

'Did you eat it?' Callum continued.

'Nathan put it in there,' Alice confirmed knowingly while Megan nudged her.

Callum tilted his head, rubbing his hand through his auburn hair. 'How?'

Lisa looked at the children, her cheeks turning pinker than those of the runners who continued to jog past. 'Ask your daddy, I think he'd like to tell you.'

Lisa smiled at Pete, who hesitated before pointing along the promenade.

'Look, I think I see Mummy.'

They all looked, straining their necks to see over and around the oncoming group of runners in their way. Lisa was about to mock Pete for attempting to avoid the question when she spotted Felicity.

'Hi, Lisa.'

Annoyed that she was being spoken to just when Felicity was in sight, Lisa turned to see Sam and Alex at her side.

'Sam, hi. I'm just looking for my friend. She's about to come by.' Lisa addressed the children as she looked back at Felicity. 'Get your banners ready, everyone, she's coming!' Lisa felt a rush of excitement.

'Great, we couldn't resist popping over to have a look. It was hard to see properly from the flat, even from the top floor.'

Lisa decided not to rise to the bait and to focus on Felicity. Nathan was at work, spending the morning at an old people's home, talking about fire safety. Sam was surely just trying to wind her up.

Felicity felt as if she was running on fumes with her energy level well and truly depleted. Along the route she had felt sick several times and had to dig deep into her reserves to keep going. She was unable to speak, her breathing was ragged, and her muscles had moved beyond burning to numb, but she was almost there! The end was in sight. The crowds, who she had felt embarrassed in front of at first, were now keeping her going with their shouts and cheers of encouragement. She was a bright red, sweaty mess, and she was pretty sure she had dried snot on her face, but she didn't care; she could see the finish line! Felicity spotted the faces of her family and their brilliant banners just a few metres from the end and knew she had to press on; walking across the finish was not an option. Her feet were no longer keeping time to a sensible running gait, and her throat and lungs were burning from the exertion, but the only thing that mattered was reaching that line. Remembering a technique shared by a runner at the 2K mark, she imagined throwing out a hook and reeling the finishing line towards her.

'Go, Mummy! Go, Mummy!'

Felicity looked at Lisa and her family as she passed them. Even Megan, who was usually the least vocal, was cheering her on. Feeling exhausted but elated, she stepped across the finishing line and jogged herself out to a halt, laughing, crying and attempting to breathe.

After they had all congratulated Felicity, and she had got her medal for running the race, they found a cup of tea for the adults and ice creams for the children. Lisa told Felicity how proud she was of her and how happy she was she was achieving her goal.

'I thought I might miss you crossing the line when Sam came and started—'

'Samantha Jones, that's it.' Felicity smiled, seemingly pleased with the declaration that meant nothing to Lisa.

'That's what?'

'That's who was standing next to you. Samantha Jones. From school. You remember, she was a couple of years below us.'

Lisa felt like she was missing something. 'I don't remember her from school; I know her because—'

'You must remember her from school. She had a big crush on Nathan. In actual fact she was one of the ones who tried to, ah hum, "comfort" him after you split up.' Looking at Lisa's face, Felicity took a breath, stopping herself from rambling further, before finishing, 'Of course he didn't go there; remember, I told you that.'

Didn't he? Lisa wondered why she hadn't remembered Sam from school. But then, of course, Flick and Nathan had been her world. She didn't have time for others. But that didn't explain why Sam herself hadn't pointed the connection out, or why Nathan hadn't said. *Why would they keep that from me?*

Chapter Nineteen

'The midwife says I'm fine to travel, so you can stop worrying. I honestly wouldn't be going to France if I thought there was a risk.' Lisa looked at Nathan and pulled one of his T-shirts out of the wardrobe. 'Can I take this one?' She was finding his clothes more comfortable than her own and had taken to wearing his T-shirts.

As Nathan nodded, she folded the shirt she had been holding and placed it in her case. 'Flick and I have been looking forward to this. It's just the weekend, and then you, Pete and the children will be there too; I promise to behave at least until you arrive.'

'Well, that's OK, then.' Nathan laughed and looked in his wardrobe with a frown. 'Half of my wardrobe is going to be there before me.'

'You don't mind, do you?'

'No, of course not. For one thing you look sexy in my T-shirts, and for another it saves me packing.'

Lisa flicked Nathan with the pair of leggings she had taken from her section of the wardrobe.

'Your aim is terrible.' Nathan laughed.

Lisa went to grab more ammunition in the shape of a pillow from the bed, but felt a tightening in her stomach as she reached across. She winced, put her hand to her bump, and attempted to steady her breathing. Trying not to reveal the concern she felt, she looked at Nathan.

'Lisa, what is it?' He was by her side, placing his arm around her shoulders.

'I just reached too far, that's all. I'm sure it's fine.'

Her breath felt too shallow. Her bump felt rigid to the touch.

'Do you want me to call someone?'

Lisa shook her head and stood still for a moment before blowing out a breath. The sensation was easing off, her muscles relaxing. 'It's OK … I think I must have pulled something as I moved.' She felt light-headed with relief as the tension left her. 'I just have to remind myself moving quickly is a thing of the past. At least until this baby arrives.' She slumped onto the edge of the bed.

Nathan sat next to her. 'Are you sure you don't want me to call someone?'

Lisa could see the concern in his eyes and wanted to reassure him. 'No, really, I think I just moved too—'

'Perhaps we should mention it while we're at the hospital?' Nathan interrupted.

Lisa thought about the signs she had missed before, but she was so much further into this pregnancy than she'd ever got with Pip. This baby was thriving and her poor muscles were just getting used to the exertion of being twenty-four weeks pregnant. 'I don't think you're supposed to discuss your pregnancy while you're visiting the maternity ward; it's just so we can look at the facilities, think about our birth plan, that sort of thing.'

'But there will be midwives, doctors, nurses there, surely?'

'I guess, being a hospital and all,' Lisa mocked before planting a kiss on Nathan's cheek.

Having got to the hospital on time, finding a parking space took a further ten minutes. Aware they were now late, Lisa went to dive out of the car but realised either the gap was too small or her belly was too big. After a couple of attempts to exit with dignity, she admitted defeat and Nathan pulled the car forward so she could get out. While he reparked, Lisa stood shaking her head at the disappointed people who had paused nearby in the hope they were vacating their space. *No, no, move along, my boyfriend is just reparking! That's right, move on, I'm just too huge to get out like a normal person!* Her cheeks flushed at the humiliation.

Once Nathan slipped annoyingly easily out of the car, Lisa took his hand. She felt nervous about seeing the maternity ward, but excited too. She looked at the hospital – an imposing edifice forming a formidable skyline against the cloudless sky. 'You know the next time we're here, it will be because I'm in labour.'

'Yes, I guess so.' Nathan squeezed her hand as they made their way inside. 'Hopefully we'll be able to park then, though I'll probably drop you by the door, save you waddling in.'

Lisa looked at him in disbelief. 'Waddling? Really?'

'Well, you'll be huge by then.'

'Huge!'

'I didn't mean huge' – Nathan elongated the word – 'forty weeks, full term.'

Lisa continued to stare at him.

'I was being nice. You'll be forty weeks and in pain.' Nathan cringed at his own words.

Lisa giggled. 'I knew what you meant; I was just letting you dig yourself a little deeper.'

Having finally discovered the maternity department on the first floor and worked out how to get inside, via an intercom, a set of double doors, and a hand-sanitiser station, Lisa and Nathan joined the back of the already formed tour group. Following largely in silence, they were led to the delivery suite, comprising of nine rooms, each with en-suite facilities and two with birthing pools. There was a lot to take in, especially when the midwife spoke about the different types of pain relief they could administer, but that the preference was always for a "normal", by which Lisa took to mean "painful", labour, in which "mum" was "up and moving". The birthing ball the midwife seemed very keen on, and even demonstrated, reminded Lisa of the orange bouncy hopper she'd had too briefly as a child, and fallen off of. *And that one had handles!*

Before they moved on to the postnatal ward, the midwife attempted to raise a smile and to reassure everyone with her don't-worry-we've-seen-it-all-before speech that did little for Lisa's confidence. She hadn't thought to be worried about being sick or, worse, pooing during labour until the well-meaning woman mentioned it. Lisa did, however, appreciate hearing about Braxton Hicks, or false contractions as the midwife had described them, and wondered if that was what she had experienced earlier. The cramping sensation the midwife mentioned was certainly an apt way to describe what Lisa had felt while reaching for the pillow.

The postnatal ward was less private than Lisa had expected, having six beds to a room. Lisa didn't take in what was said as she found herself drawn to looking at the new mums with their babies, hardly daring to believe that would be her in sixteen weeks' time. When Nathan nudged her with the words, 'you'll never manage that', she didn't know what he was referring to, until the midwife looked at them and reiterated that the two-small-bags policy was for everyone's benefit, as space was tight. Lisa felt herself blush before responding, 'Of course.' And then wondered how she would fit all she needed for herself and the baby in anything less than a very large suitcase, or two.

When the tour was finally over, Lisa welcomed the cool evening air that contrasted to the warm, stale air of the hospital. 'Will you still love me when I'm huge and waddling?'

'Of course I will.'

As they walked towards the car park pay station, Lisa remained in a contemplative mood. She was very happy to be pregnant; to be with Nathan and carrying his baby was more than she dared to hope for when she moved home from London. But as the pregnancy progressed and the things happening to her body increasingly seemed beyond her control, the more it dawned on her how quickly her relationship with Nathan was changing. The period of getting reacquainted, after being apart for eleven years, was moving at a rapid speed. Pregnancy, and especially birth, left little mystery between a couple – it really was a bare-all situation, at least for the woman. 'What about if I'm sick or poo during labour?'

'Well, that will be pushing it,' Nathan teased before noticing Lisa's unsmiling expression. 'Of course I will,' he added more reassuringly with a squeeze of her hand.

'Good because, technically, as you got me pregnant, it will all be your fault.'

Nathan raised his eyebrows. 'Oh really?'

Lisa liked the amusement she saw in his eyes as they glinted in what was left of the evening sun. 'Yes!'

'Well, I think you helped me on that front, but I can take it. You can blame me for everything.'

'Oh, I will.' Lisa giggled as Nathan pulled her into a kiss.

'That'll be what got you both here in the first place!'

Lisa and Nathan turned to see Dom standing next to them. In greeting, Lisa hugged and kissed him, while Nathan said hello.

'We've been on a tour of the maternity ward. It's all getting a bit real now.' Lisa blew out a breath.

'I should hope it's real; if not, you need to cut back on the roast dinners!'

Nathan's eyes went wide; a probably-best-not-to-go-there gesture.

Dom grinned as Lisa swiped playfully at his arm.

'Cheeky bugger! So why are you here? You don't look like you're working.' Lisa motioned to Dom's jeans and T-shirt.

'I brought Gran over.'

'Is Winnie all right?' Lisa had seen Winnie just the day before, but she hadn't mentioned going to hospital.

'Yes, she's visiting a friend. Maureen, I think she said.'

'Maureen with the Yorkshire terrier, that Maureen?' Lisa asked, remembering meeting Maureen when she had accompanied Winnie on a visit to her local church.

'Yes, that must be her. She tripped over the dog.'

'Oh no! Poor Tubby, was he OK?'

'I think you're meant to check on the person before the dog.' Nathan laughed.

'Ha, I've met Maureen. But from what I remember, she and Winnie weren't exactly friendly towards each other.'

Dom shrugged. 'You know Gran, she likes to help an injured soul.'

Lisa blushed, remembering how Winnie had entrusted Jack to her when she first moved back to Littlehampton, not because she had proven pet-sitting skills but because Winnie had recognised how lost and lonely Lisa had been back then. 'Yes, she's good at that. I hope Maureen appreciates the visit.'

'I hope so too. Though I think Gran has plans to recommend your pet-sitting services while she's got a captive audience.'

'Oh, bless her.' Lisa smiled.

'She won't be about for the next week though,' Nathan interjected.

'That's right, Flick and I are off to France tomorrow—'

'Gran said. Half your luck. I'm on holiday this week, but haven't made plans. I think Gran's lining up a list of jobs.'

'You'd be welcome along. Nathan, Pete and the children are joining us after the weekend. We're celebrating our thirtieths and staying at my parents' chalet in the Alps. The more the merrier. We can make room for one more.' Lisa looked between Dom and Nathan, wondering if she should have checked first.

'I couldn't gatecrash.' Dom looked at Nathan.

'You'd be welcome, but I'm not sure Pete's got space in the car—' Nathan began.

'I could bike down. I haven't given the motorcycle a good run for a while.'

Lisa could tell Dom was excited at the prospect.

'With a couple of stops, it's about thirteen hours, a bit more than a good run.' She welcomed his enthusiasm but wanted him to be sure he knew what he was letting himself in for.

'I could do it in about nine, I reckon.'

'What have you got?' Nathan asked.

'MV Agusta F3, it—'

Nathan took a breath, but Lisa spoke first.

'What will you do if it rains?'

Dom and Nathan shared an eye roll that told Lisa she had said something foolish even before the words *get wet* were said in unison.

'OK.' Lisa held up her hands, conceding it wasn't the most technical of questions. 'So, do you think you can make it?'

'If you really don't mind me tagging along.'

'And will Winnie mind … about the jobs? I don't want to be in trouble.' Not wanting to upset Winnie, Lisa thought she should check.

'I'll get some things done before I leave, to make Gran happy, and join you on Sunday night. How does that sound?'

'Really?' Lisa was excited at the thought of having Dom along too. He had met Felicity when Lisa took her to meet Jack, and the two had got on instantly, so she was sure she wouldn't mind.

'If you're sure.' Dom looked between Lisa and Nathan again.

'Of course we are.' Lisa squeezed Nathan's hand.

'To be honest, it will be good to have you along. Lisa had a few twinges earlier,' Nathan added.

Dom looked at Lisa, concerned. 'You're OK now, aren't you?'

'Fine. I think it was Braxton Hicks. Something I've learnt tonight.'

'Take it easy though, won't you? After—'

'Of course I will.' Lisa cut Dom short and leaned in to hug him goodbye with the promise of texting him once she was home with her parents' address in France and any other details that sprang to mind that he might need to know.

Nathan said his goodbyes and stepped aside to pay for the parking.

Dom hugged Lisa goodbye once more. 'I'm glad you two had your talk and that you look so bloomin' happy! Didn't I tell you it would be fine?'

As they walked to the car, Lisa couldn't help but notice a tic of tension at Nathan's jaw and hoped she had done the right thing asking Dom to join them in France. Luckily the car next to them had moved, and she was able to get in without difficulty.

'You didn't mind me asking Dom along, did you?'

'No, of course not.'

'Then what's up?'

Nathan met her gaze. 'What talk was Dom referring to?'

'When?' Lisa felt her cheeks blush.

'You know when. He said he was pleased we had our talk. What talk was he referring to?'

Her mouth felt dry as her throat tightened. 'The one about Pip.' Her voice came out on a wobble. 'I spoke to Dom about wanting to talk to you.'

'So you told him first?' Nathan glanced at her, hurt evident in his eyes.

'Yes, but Flick knew too. Dom's my friend—'

'Now. He's your friend now.'

'He's never been anything more.' Lisa thought about when she had first met Dom, how the two of them had flirted with each other and even gone on a date or two before she told Dom she had feelings for Nathan, and he had told her while he had had girlfriends, his preference was for men.

'Flick knew. I told her. It was no different.' Even to her own ears that sounded weak. The circumstances under which she had told her two friends about losing Pip were very different; Felicity had listened and been a comfort at a time when she needed it, Dom had been a sounding board to gauge what Nathan's reaction might be.

'Really?' Nathan looked at her, incredulous, before driving out of the car park.

Chapter Twenty

Lisa checked her bag for her ticket and passport. So as not to waste a moment of their weekend, she and Felicity were setting off on the Friday. They had decided to taxi to Gatwick and then fly to Geneva airport, hiring a car from there to take them the final leg of the journey. Pete, Nathan and the children were going to drive down together to meet them so they'd have enough vehicle space for everyone when it came to going out during the week. The plan was that at the end of the week Flick would return with her family, and Nathan would fly back with Lisa. They had worked it all out perfectly, and Lisa had been looking forward to the trip for months.

But after her evening with Nathan, which resulted in her lying to escape the atmosphere between them, she felt like calling the holiday off. Telling him she needed to go back to her mum's for items she'd forgotten and that it was probably easier for the taxi to pick her up from there was a return to her old form. *Why face a situation when you can run from it?* But she had been tired, frustrated at herself for unthinkingly hurting Nathan and, if she was honest, preferred to avoid confrontation after her years with Ben.

Felicity was beyond excited about the trip; she had bought Globetrotting Percy Pig sweets from M&S for them to share in the taxi, and was playing Robbie Williams's greatest hits on her phone – her and Lisa's favourite from their teenage years – at a volume Lisa found a bit much considering she had hardly slept. Lisa attempted to put on a smile and asked how Pete and the children were. When Felicity explained how they had waved her off with homemade French flags and had learnt to say 'au revoir' and 'bon voyage', Lisa knew she had to get herself together. She couldn't let her issues with Nathan spoil their trip. Clearing the air, or at least apologising, suddenly felt essential.

'Flick, can we do a quick stop off at Nathan's? I need to just run in. I won't be long.'

Felicity asked the taxi driver if they had time, before looking back at Lisa. 'Have you forgotten something?'

'Not really. I just need to see Nathan. I promise to be quick.'

'You two, seriously! You'll only be apart for the weekend.'

'I know, I just really need to. Is that OK?' Lisa felt gripped by the urgent need to sort the situation before she got on the plane.

When they reached Nathan's, Lisa was undoing her seatbelt before the driver had a chance to stop the car. She leaned over and hugged her friend. 'Thanks for this. I won't be long.'

She went inside and up the stairs as fast as her pregnant state would allow. Reaching the top floor, more out of breath than she would have liked, Lisa unlocked the door and went inside, calling Nathan's name. There was no answer. Feeling deflated, she looked around. His breakfast things were in the sink, but his bed was made, and he wasn't in the bathroom.

Noticing Uno lying in the centre of his wooden cat bridge – one of the gadgets she was reviewing for *Paws About Town* magazine – Lisa beckoned him. Uno looked at her, torn between his comfortable position and the possibility of some fuss or, even better, some food. The bridge was clearly proving a hit, and she hoped her report on it would go down as well with her editor as the one on the dog lead had. She had also reviewed a less successful 'Dirty Doggy

Bag' she had attempted to zip Jack in after a muddy walk and had received a Pet Cam she had yet to fathom how to use. The payment for the articles so far had been enough for her to enjoy a spending spree at Mothercare.

Eventually, Uno slunk across the wooden slats of the rope bridge that stretched between two shelves, and thudded down at her feet. Lisa picked him up, rewarding him by rubbing around his ears and generally making a fuss of him. Feeling the cat in her arms made her feel connected to Nathan. 'Where is he, Uno?'

Lisa thought about writing a note, but apologising in a note wouldn't clear the air in the way speaking to him face-to-face would; it felt only one step better than sending a text, which she had already discounted.

Giving Uno a few treats before saying goodbye, Lisa left. She knew she had to put on a smile and throw herself into her weekend with Felicity. Her friend deserved that. This weekend was about them – the holiday they had always planned but not taken as teenagers. Deciding that phoning Nathan was as near as she could get to speaking to him in person, Lisa took out her phone and pressed to call him before setting off down the stairs. As she passed Sam's door, she couldn't help but notice it was slightly ajar. She didn't know if it had been that way as she'd gone up the stairs; she'd been too intent on getting to Nathan's to look. But it wasn't only the door being ajar that was drawing her attention now, it was the fact she could hear a phone ringing, and she was pretty sure it was Nathan's ringtone.

She stopped at the door. Edging closer, she pushed it slightly, increasing the gap as she strained to listen. Looking at her phone, Lisa pressed to end the call. The ringing stopped. She held her breath. The only audible sounds were the rush of blood at her ears and the thud of her own heartbeat. She pressed to call again, wondering, hoping that it was a coincidence. The ringing started once more. She quickly ended the call.

Of course, there were many reasons why Nathan could be in Sam's flat: he was technically her landlord, they were friends and ... *and what?* Lisa felt there was something she was missing. The thought had been nagging at the back of her mind for some time, and it frustrated her. She didn't like to think Nathan and Sam were sharing a secret she wasn't party to. Not because she didn't trust Nathan, but because Sam's behaviour and the things she said made Lisa question her motives. She had no real reason, but her instincts told her not to trust her. The timing for Nathan to be in Sam's flat wasn't great either. Lisa didn't want to have to speak to him in front of Sam, and if she were honest, she didn't like the fact he was there, that morning, after they'd had a disagreement. The idea caused jealousy to twist her stomach into knots and claw at her rational thoughts.

Knocking on the door, she waited. When there was no response, she walked inside. It was small – kitchen, bathroom, lounge and one bedroom. A glance from the hallway told her nobody was there. Although it was Nathan's building and his furnishings, she knew she was trespassing, but being driven by an overwhelming desire to know why Nathan's phone was inside, she couldn't bring herself to leave. Not yet.

Sam and Alex hadn't brought many belongings with them, but there were personal touches evident all around: Lego, discarded trainers, an Xbox and games, a vase of flowers, washing drying on an airer – including underwear, which made Lisa wish her maternity briefs had been chosen for sex appeal as opposed to comfort – and the musky scent of Sam.

Lisa felt every nerve telling her she should leave, that she was going to be caught any minute. But now she'd crossed the threshold and was as far as the lounge, curiosity was drawing her deeper into Sam's world. About to ring Nathan's phone again, Lisa spotted it on the table by the window. She walked over and picked it up. The movement caused the screen to light up, revealing notifications registering her missed calls and a picture of her and Nathan, taken in France at Christmas. Seeing Nathan's face made her feel as guilty as if he were in the room catching her in the act of snooping. She cleared the notifications and put the phone down.

Guilt seeping into her nerves, she realised how visible she was in the window and dived back behind the curtain. Peering round to see if anyone had seen her, Lisa noticed two figures playing tennis on the courts opposite. It was Nathan and Alex. She hadn't noticed them as she'd got out of the car; they'd been hidden by the line of trees. But she could see them now, laughing and running around. *So where's Sam?*

Aware that Sam could be en route to her flat caused Lisa to panic. Now that her common sense had returned and was screaming for her to leave, she ducked back out of sight of the window and headed for the door, her breathing rapid. In her haste her foot caught in the handle of a small grey rucksack she hadn't noticed next to the sofa. *Bugger!* Bending to free herself and pick up the items that had scattered from it, Lisa swore again. Her chances of not being caught were diminishing with every second that passed.

Lisa stuffed the items back in the bag – pens, tissues, Sam's driving licence, a bottle of Victoria's Secret's perfume called Sexy Sparkle, *of course*, a half full and now extremely fizzy bottle of Coke, and a hairbrush. *How orderly could they have been?* Sweeping her hand under the sofa, Lisa checked for anything she had missed. Feeling a small cube, she pulled it out. As it came in to view, her breath hitched and her vision beyond anything but the blue box, indented with a silver inlay square, blurred as she focused on it intently. She had seen it before, not for almost twelve years, but she recognised it. How could she not?

Her hands shaking, Lisa opened the lid. It squeaked before clicking and lodging into place – open like a clam holding a precious pearl. There, inside was the ring. Her ring. Or at least it would have been her ring if she had said yes. Having not seen it since her prom night, Lisa stared at it. It was beautiful. She had no idea if the gems were real, but the six-prong centre stone flanked by smaller side stones looked like diamonds and glistened in the light as her hand trembled. Seeing the ring now, Lisa wondered why she had ever found the sight of it so terrifying. Her heart thudded as an image of Nathan holding it out to her came to mind. She blinked, attempting to force herself to stay in the moment and decide what to do.

Although she had wondered, she had never asked Nathan what had happened to the ring. And now here it was. Lisa didn't know if it had come from Sam's bag and fallen on the floor or if it had been lying there lost under the sofa. How, when or why that might have happened in either case baffled her. *Why would Sam have my ... Nathan's ring?* Her phone vibrating in her hand made her jump, and she almost dropped it. Lisa looked to see a message from Felicity telling her to get a move on. Realising that had been her intention before she discovered the ring, she snapped the box closed and glanced around the room. Nathan's phone was hopefully as she had found it. She put the bag on the floor in the vicinity of where it had been, clutched the blue box containing the ring in her hand, and left, leaving the door slightly ajar as she went.

As Lisa attempted to run down the stairs towards the front door, she could feel a tightening in her stomach. *Braxton Hicks!* She placed her hand over her firm bump; her skin felt taut. She breathed in and out, focusing on pushing on down the stairs despite the quickening in her muscles.

Once at the door she hurried back to the taxi. Felicity leaned across and opened the door.

'What is it? You look awful.'

'I'm fine. Let's just go.' Lisa nodded to the driver, who was awaiting confirmation that he could pull away.

'What happened? You look like you've committed a murder.'

Lisa noticed the driver turn his eyes to her in the mirror. Lisa clenched her teeth as she reached and put her seatbelt on. The tension in her stomach started to ease, and she hissed, 'Of course I haven't.' She felt the ring box in her pocket. *Theft perhaps? Surely, it can't be stealing if it was always meant to be mine, can it?*

Chapter Twenty-One

The temperature in England had been mild, but France, in May, was hot – hotter than Lisa had imagined. As Felicity drove them along the twisty roads up in to the mountains, Lisa wished she had worn lighter clothes – in material and colour. Her black leggings were absorbing the heat of the sun through the windscreen of the hire car, making her too warm despite the best efforts of the Skoda Fabia's air conditioning.

Felicity looked awestruck at the dramatic scenery as stretches of grass broken by the occasional chalet or barn, forests of pine, and snow-capped mountains flanked the road. 'It's beautiful, breath-taking. Is it just me, or is the sky bluer here?'

'I think it's just that we can see more of it, fewer houses, bigger scenery. Does that make sense?' Lisa peered through the windscreen.

'No. I think it's bluer.'

Lisa laughed, enjoying seeing Felicity so animated, and relieved that her friend with a self-professed penchant for beach holidays was taking so readily to a break in the mountains.

'Look, cows!' Felicity swung the car on to the grass verge and pressed to lower her window.

A few of the medium-sized brown and white cows, looking as if they had stepped off the wrapper of a bar of Milka chocolate, glanced up inquisitively and sauntered over. The bells attached to thick leather straps around their necks clanged repetitively as they moved. The rings through their soft pink noses and the fact they had no udders suggested they were bullocks, but Lisa didn't say. Instead she soaked up the noise as it resonated on the cool breeze, looked into their dark enquiring eyes and admired their long eyelashes.

Felicity put her hands on her hips and took a big breath. 'The children will love these. I can't wait to … arghh, I'm at it already. This weekend is meant to be about us, a little oasis in the desert of real-life responsibilities, and here I am getting excited about cows and wanting to show the children.'

'Don't worry about it. I love them too.'

'My children?'

'Of course, but I meant the cows.'

Felicity laughed and took out her phone to take the first of many holiday pictures.

When they pulled up outside Lisa's parents' three-storey chalet, nestled above the village of Samoëns, Felicity's eyes boggled. 'Wow! It's beautiful.'

'And it is all ours, at least until Sunday evening!'

The pair shared a satisfied smile before getting out of the car.

The air was clear. The only sounds were the chirping of crickets as they stridulated in the surrounding grass, and the faint rush of meltwater tumbling down the face of a distant mountain. As the two of them stood soaking in the view, Lisa couldn't help but compare the verdant late spring surroundings with the winter landscape she had seen during her visit in December when snow had dominated the view.

Now the sky was a crisp light blue and cotton wool clouds hung low across the lush mountains. Lisa could see the ski runs she had watched being prepared in the winter, now slick carpets of green streaking down between the trees. The ski lifts sat idle. To her left a craggy mountain untouched by vegetation stretched higher into the sky. Its snow cap glistened as the sun touched but didn't penetrate it.

'Right, let's get this holiday started.' Felicity walked to the rear of the car, popping open the small boot. As her bag was less than half the size of Lisa's, she passed it to her.

'I don't know what you've got in here.' Felicity groaned as she lifted Lisa's case out.

'I didn't know what the weather would be like, or what I would be comfortable in. Besides, I'm packing for two.'

'You know that's not actually a thing until the baby arrives, don't you?'

Lisa laughed. 'I meant me and Nathan. I've stolen half his wardrobe.' *And the engagement ring he once tried to give me.* Seeing her case, where she had slipped the ring before baggage drop at the airport, made guilt pulsate through her once more. Lisa recalled being in Sam's flat and her snap decision to take the ring. With the distance of time and over six hundred miles, she couldn't believe her actions; the things she had done played through her mind as if watching somebody else. Despite being tempted many times on the journey, she hadn't confessed to Felicity. Lisa already knew her advice would be to speak to Nathan. She even conceded it was the sensible thing to do, but with Nathan in England and the weekend ahead to focus on with Felicity, Lisa was happy to remain in denial about the need for that conversation, at least for the next two days.

As Lisa rummaged in her bag for the key her mum had entrusted her with, she looked at Felicity's bag at her feet. 'How have you packed so little?'

'I've packed my good friends the Molton Browns, Penny and Percy Pig, a couple of maxi-dresses, and a swimsuit for the hot tub. Oh, and a few essentials like sun cream and underwear.'

'You're here for a week!'

'And Pete is bringing the rest.' Felicity smiled.

Lisa opened the front door and motioned for Flick to go in first.

She put down the case she had lifted over the threshold and blew out a breath. 'Wow again! Lisa, this is amazing. I knew I should have kept in contact with your parents when you buggered off after our prom!' Felicity giggled and spun around in awe.

By the time Sunday evening arrived, Lisa and Felicity were completely chilled out and felt they had taken relaxation to a whole new level. Felicity sat in the hot tub sipping wine while Lisa was drinking blackcurrant squash, and eating Maltesers, with her feet in a paddling pool they had bought at the local supermarché. The once red umbrella, they had put up for protection from the hot sun, was weathered in stripes; its ornate wrought-iron base took centre stage between the two of them on the terrace. The table, chairs and barbecue sat idly waiting for the arrival of the others, who would no doubt put them all to good use. A lizard, no larger than Lisa's palm, flitted about the terrace, pausing mid-motion each time they looked directly at it, as if it were playing a game of Sly Fox.

Lisa stretched her arms above her head, attempting to shift the baby into a more comfortable position. 'I'm here to celebrate my thirtieth. I can't drink, I can't go in the hot tub, beyond the protection of this umbrella it is too bloody hot, and I could not be happier.' She raised her glass to Felicity. 'We're finally on our girl trip, just the two of us, I'm so pleased we found each other again, and ... hello, who is that?'

The sound of tyres against gravel drew their attention

towards the driveway, but being at the back of the building, they couldn't see who was there.

'It's too early for Pete. He said they'd be at least another hour.'

'And that's not a motorbike, so it's not Dom.'

Felicity stood up and grabbed her towel. 'Whoever it is can't see me like this. I've got enough rolls to open a boulangerie.'

Lisa giggled. 'Wait, don't leave me.' Realising Felicity was heading inside, she swung her legs out of the paddling pool, hurriedly rubbed her feet on a towel, and followed, closing the patio door behind them before panicking about the fact they were dripping water on her mum's floor. From their vantage point behind the sofa, the two women watched as a suave man wandered round the garden. Dressed in a smart-casual style, he wore navy fitted jeans; an untucked pale blue, tailored shirt; and tan, leather-weave jute loafers without socks. His tanned skin, along with his dark hair, which occasionally flopped across his sunglasses, made Lisa think he was French.

'Who the hell is Monsieur Hottie?' Flick asked. 'Do you think he's a thief? The place is supposed to be empty until your parents return.'

'No. The hire car is on the driveway, it's broad daylight and … well, look at him.'

'Perhaps he's—'

'A very posh gardener?'

With a couple of athletic strides, the man ascended the steps of the terrace. He walked towards the door and lifted his sunglasses before knocking and peering in.

Lisa and Felicity attempted to stand still, but the fact he lifted his hand in a single wave and offered a smile revealing a fine set of white teeth made it obvious he had seen them.

'Well, now we look stupid hiding behind here.' Felicity nudged Lisa towards the door.

'I can't go. I'm only in a T-shirt and pants. At least you're in a swimsuit and towel.' Lisa pulled the bottom of Nathan's T-shirt down, attempting to cover her bump and knickers.

Felicity edged forward. 'What if he's dangerous?'

'Nobody that good-looking could be dangerous.'

Felicity looked admonishingly at Lisa. 'And that's why he's dangerous! You'd better stay behind me.'

'Wait!' As they were about to open the door, Lisa grabbed Felicity's arm and whispered, 'Can you speak French?'

Felicity matched Lisa's hushed tones. 'I can say my name, age, where I live, and Jean Paul works in the garden.'

Lisa looked at her, dumbfounded, before they both giggled.

'You cover me and I'll speak,' Lisa affirmed.

Felicity opened the door. Both women took in the sight of the man's handsome features. His ice-blue eyes contrasted with his tanned skin, dark hair and the fine stubble that outlined his heart-shaped face.

'*Bonsoir.*'

From her position behind Felicity, Lisa spoke, asking, in French, if she could help him in what she hoped was a calm steady voice, but reminded her of her mum attempting to be posh. With an amused grin the man introduced himself, speaking English with a soft, intoxicating French accent, as Florian. He explained that he was the son of their nearest neighbour and that he taught Lisa's mum's art class. As a favour to Lisa's parents, his father had prepared the hot tub for their arrival, and he was there to check on the chemical balance of the water.

Satisfactory explanations having been provided, Lisa and

Felicity ran to find some more suitable clothes while Florian directed his attention to the hot tub.

'I think Flor-i-an' – Felicity spoke his name with a faux French accent – 'did something to my chemical balance.'

'No wonder my mother has taken so well to her art classes.' Lisa laughed as she pulled on a pair of shorts and left them undone to accommodate her bump. 'Do you think we should offer him a drink, being a family friend and all?'

Felicity slid on her maxi-dress. 'Diet Coke, maybe?'

'Behave. We will not be encouraging Florian to take off his top like the Diet Coke man. You're a happily married woman, and I'm—' Lisa pulled Nathan's T-shirt down, attempting to cover the open button of her shorts '—very pregnant.' As she let go of the hem, it sprang back up as if to prove the point.

Hurrying back down, Lisa and Flick paused at the bottom of the wooden staircase. Looking across the lounge towards the terrace, the two women tilted their heads in unison, watching from their vantage point as Florian laughed and chatted to a newly arrived Dom. Dressed in black Alpinestars leathers, looking unshaven, with his dark hair slick from where he had removed his helmet, Dom was smiling and seemed obscurely interested in the workings of the hot tub for someone who had just completed an at-least-eight-hour journey.

'Look at the two of them. Is it just me, or is there more chemistry going on out there than just checking the pH balance in the hot tub?'

'I'm no expert, but that does look like flirting, doesn't it?'

'Mirrored body language, eye contact, hair flicking – it's flirting,' Felicity agreed before adding, 'That'll explain it?'

'Explain what?'

'Why Florian kept his eyes on our faces while we were half-naked.'

Lisa laughed. 'Trust you to notice that. Maybe he was just being polite?'

Felicity gestured towards the terrace, where Dom was unzipping his leathers down to his waist, revealing a fitted base layer clinging to muscles being more than admired by Florian's drifting ice-blue eyes. 'Sure he was!'

Catching each other's eye, Lisa and Felicity giggled and headed outside. Lisa welcomed Dom with a hug and wondered if the heat in his cheeks was from his long ride or his encounter with Florian.

'Dom, you're here. You know Flick, and I can see you've already met Florian, he's an artist.' Lisa looked at Dom and wiggled her eyebrows, holding back the 'good with his hands' she wanted to add.

The flush on Dom's cheeks spread. 'Yes … he, um … was just … you know what, it's really hot out here. Do you mind if I get unpacked and hit the shower?'

'No, of course not.' Lisa smiled. 'I'll show you where you'll be sleeping and where to put your things.' *Oh, this could be perfect – Monsieur Hottie, meet Captain Not-Quite-So-Calm-After-All!*

Chapter Twenty-Two

Nathan, Pete and the children arrived as the blue sky of earlier in the day was replaced by grey clouds threatening rain. While it was still warm, the crickets had fallen silent and thunder rumbled over the mountains. Lisa welcomed Nathan's hug. His lips upon hers made all thoughts of their tense parting disappear. She watched as he greeted Dom with a smile, and the happy acceptance of the beer he offered. Having not cleared the air before she left, Lisa had been dreading an atmosphere and was pleased to see Nathan wasn't going to let his feelings about Dom knowing about Pip spoil the holiday.

As they brought their luggage from the car to the chalet, the quiet of the past two days was replaced by an array of voices all talking at the same time. While Lisa had enjoyed her weekend with Felicity, she welcomed the new chaos. Compared to the loneliness she had felt a year ago, she was aware how lucky she was to have Nathan and her friends around her. In the back of her mind she knew she had to speak to Nathan about the engagement ring, but that all seemed so irrelevant in the happy holiday atmosphere.

Felicity was beaming at the sight of children and swooped them into an embrace. 'Oh, I've missed you. You know I love you bigger than the world!'

'I love you this much!' Fred splayed his little arms as far open as he could.

'I love you to the moon and back,' shouted Callum.

'I love you to infinity.' Megan smiled, having trumped her brothers.

'I love you bigger than a tapeworm!' Alice declared.

As they all laughed and Alice began an indignant explanation as to why that wasn't funny, Lisa knew she had a wonderful week ahead. *Let the madness begin.*

Friday came around too quickly. They had spent whole days at Lac Bleu in nearby Morillon enjoying the mountain lake, quiet beach, ice cream and stunning views. Nathan had been parapenting and encouraged Dom and Pete to go white-water rafting with him. Lisa was pleased Felicity had found time to run most mornings before the heat of the day took hold. Flick and Pete had also taken a helicopter ride over the mountains in celebration of her thirtieth birthday, before having a meal in a local restaurant, making the most of the fact that holidaying with friends meant holidaying with babysitter benefits.

Lisa opened her eyes and stretched. The sun was coming through the curtains. She could hear the children playing, the kettle boiling, and Flick and Pete chatting in the kitchen.

'Happy thirtieth birthday.' Nathan's voice was thick with sleep as he leaned up on his pillow.

Lisa turned to look at him and smiled, enjoying the warmth of his firm chest as she leaned into him. 'Thank you.'

'I am looking forward to today—' he kissed her nose '— and getting you all to my—'

A knock at the door interrupted Nathan's words and the trail his hand was making down Lisa's side. He rolled back on to his own pillow with a mock exaggerated sigh.

Lisa giggled as she sat up, pulling the sheet over herself. Time alone wasn't easy in a chalet full of people. 'Come in.'

Flick stuck her head round the door. 'Happy birthday! I've contained them for an hour, so when I heard voices, I thought you wouldn't mind—'

Before Felicity could finish her sentence, Fred pushed past her. 'Happy birthday, Lisa!'

The rest of Felicity's children – who were holding handfuls of wild flowers, homemade cards and pastries on a plate – followed. Felicity held out a cup of coffee for Nathan and a glass of squash for Lisa. 'Hope we're not interrupting.'

'I told her she'd be interrupting.' Pete's voice came from the hallway.

'She is definitely interrupting!' Nathan called back, with laughter in his tone.

'Not at all.' Lisa took the flowers and set the pastries aside before encouraging the children on to the bed and reading her cards enthusiastically. As her phone began to ring, Lisa saw that her mum was FaceTiming. 'Who wants to speak to my mummy?'

The chaos in the room increasing, Nathan slipped out of bed in his black boxer briefs. Felicity teasingly averted her eyes as he put on a T-shirt before she passed him his coffee and he went to find Pete. Lisa and the children watched as her mum and dad sang to her and offered birthday wishes. The children took it in turns to say hello and to share what their favourite part of the holiday had been. Felicity chatted to Lisa's parents about how grateful she was to have had the week in their beautiful chalet. Once the call was over, the children ran to get ready for their day of adventure tree climbing.

As Lisa sat back in bed, watching and feeling her baby move, Dom knocked.

'I hear the birthday girl is awake.'

Lisa smiled as he entered the room. 'Awake and spoilt already.'

'So you don't want this, then?' Dom held out a present.

'It would be rude of me not to take it after you've gone to the trouble—'

Dom passed the gift and Lisa opened it.

'It's from me and Gran.'

'Wow! Dom, it's great, thank you.' Lisa looked at the cuddly penguin, a little perplexed.

Dom sat next to her on the bed. 'I was on one of those websites that gives you ideas for presents. Skydiving and paintballing were out of the question.' Dom motioned to her bump. 'I wasn't sure you were the spa day sort.'

Lisa went to protest but then thought about how Dom usually saw her – in her work clothes and covered in dog slobber, or worse.

'And then I happened upon sponsoring an animal.' Dom leaned over and pulled out a sponsorship certificate from the box that had contained the penguin. 'So I got you a penguin.'

'It's perfect. Who doesn't love penguins?'

'Gran, apparently; she called me a daft beggar and pointed out that a rescue dog would have made more sense.'

Lisa giggled. Trust Winnie to think logically and not to hold back when it came to criticism.

'But when I pointed out, as it is at a local zoo, you can take your baby and show him or her your penguin, I won her round.'

'Dom, that's so lovely.'

Dom smiled, gave Lisa a birthday kiss on the cheek, and stood up. 'There's no good reason for it being a penguin, by the way, other than it was called Jack. You could have ended up with one of those big-bottomed monkeys.'

Lisa laughed.

'Florian's outside.' Nathan stood in the doorway, where he had been watching Lisa and Dom.

As Dom said his goodbyes, Lisa noticed the smile that betrayed his anticipation of the day ahead. He and Florian were going sightseeing. The two of them had spent several evenings together, as Lisa had encouraged Florian to join them for barbecues and drinks. As everyone else retired to the house, Florian and Dom had increasingly stayed on the terrace chatting until late. Lisa wasn't sure how intimate they had become, as Nathan prevented her from spying over the balcony, but it was obvious they were enjoying each other's company. It might only have the potential to be a holiday fling, but Lisa was pleased to see Dom so happy.

As Dom left the room, Nathan opened the balcony door a little, letting in the morning air before walking over to Lisa.

'I'm sorry I was an arse about Dom before. I know he's your friend and—'

Lisa felt a rush of relief at Nathan broaching the subject. 'No, I'm sorry. You were right to feel hurt. I should have told you first.'

'Really, it doesn't matter. You needed someone to talk to and he was there. After Ben, I get why it wouldn't have been easy for you. But I want you to know you can talk to me. You can trust me, Lisa.'

Lisa saw the sincerity in his eyes. 'Thank you, and I do know that. Really I do.' *I just need to get better at reminding myself of that.* She slid her hand to his neck and moved closer for a kiss.

Nathan kissed her back, making a low growl in response. 'Finally, I get you to myself.' He slid under the sheet and pulled her closer to him, wrapping her in his arms.

Lisa leaned into Nathan's firm chest, feeling content. 'Thank you for a lovely birthday.' She looked at her bracelet, wondering if her present from Nathan might be a new charm. She knew this holiday with her friends would always be a special memory.

Nathan kissed her neck. 'It's only just begun.'

Lisa turned towards him, her hands slipping under his T-shirt as she enjoyed the feel and flex of his every move.

Chapter Twenty-Three

As they lay naked, with the exception of Lisa's bracelet on her wrist, covered only by the cotton sheet, the chalet was quiet. It was just the two of them. Felicity and her family had set off for the day, and Dom's motorbike, complete with Florian riding pillion, had roared its way into the distance some time ago. Lisa wondered about talking to Nathan, but the morning had started in such a perfect way and Nathan had made promises of the day ahead being even better. She didn't want to spoil that. It wasn't every day a person turned thirty, after all. Instead she lay there, her cheeks pink, her breathing ragged, feeling perfectly sated. The breeze from the open balcony door cooled her while she listened to the sounds of the crickets heralding the warm day, and the rush of the meltwater falling in the distance.

After a breakfast on the terrace of the pastries the children had given Lisa earlier that morning, Nathan said they should get ready. While Lisa didn't know where they were going, she soon recognised the road from Samoëns to Sixt-Fer-à-Cheval and the dramatic scenery as they drove towards the area of natural beauty. An eagle swooped high above them. The meltwater rushed along the stream next to the road. As Nathan took the turning to Cascade du Rouget, Lisa knew they were heading to the magnificent waterfall. The road twisted its way upward. As they crossed narrow bridges, Lisa opened her window and could hear the force within the constantly rushing water.

'It's amazing, isn't it? Can we get out?'

Nathan gestured to the road ahead. 'There's a place to stop just up here.'

'Have you been exploring?'

'I found it on my phone. I wanted to take you somewhere special.'

Lisa put her hand on Nathan's thigh. 'Thank you.'

As they turned the corner, the full spectacle of the eighty-metre waterfall came into view, stretching high above them and disappearing below the road before continuing on the other side. The nearer they drove, the more spray covered the windscreen. Pulling in to park just beyond the falls, Nathan reached for their coats.

'We'll need these.'

Lisa was pleased he had thought to bring them. It was a hot day, but the temperature, even as they opened the car doors, was obviously several degrees lower than it had been at the chalet. As they walked towards the waterfall, the chill in the air increased. Nathan put his arm around her. Lisa giggled as they walked into the spray and it made her hair and skin wet – like misty rain, or as her Granny Blake had always called it, wet rain. The sound of the surging water was incredible as it tumbled over two huge steps in the mountainside. It was a feast for the senses. They took photographs, posing with the spectacle behind them.

Having experienced the magnificence of the Cascade du Rouget at close quarters, they walked up a rough side slope, towards a café where they could admire the view and dry off in the warmth of the sun, with an ice cream. Taking a table outside, they watched others park up and walk as near as they could to the waterfall; some even took the path that climbed up the side for a closer view, appearing as tiny figures alongside the second of the steps in the mountain.

'The website said it completely freezes in winter, and when the conditions are right, you can climb up the ice. It's hard to imagine now, isn't it?'

Lisa looked at Nathan; his smile and enthusiasm were

youthful as he soaked in the view. 'We'll have to come back in the winter so we can see it. My parents will be here then too. We can bring the baby to France for Christmas.'

'Maybe. Though you might want to have the baby's first Christmas at home.'

Lisa smiled. She wasn't sure whether Nathan meant his home or her parents' home in England. Sorting out where she and the baby would be living was another conversation she and Nathan needed to have. She had watched Flick and Pete all week; they operated well together. Of course they had the odd disagreement and quick quarrel, but mostly, so much was well established about their routines and relationship they made it look easy, probably easier than it was. Lisa recalled something Winnie had once told her, 'Don't judge your insides by others' outsides.' Like many of Winnie's sayings, Lisa had found it cryptic at the time, but she felt she was starting to understand it.

Nathan took Lisa's hand, stroking across the back of it with his thumb. 'You OK? You look miles away.'

'Yes, of course. I'm right here, with you.'

Lisa's gaze met his blue eyes.

'Good.'

Nathan hesitated and Lisa wondered if he was holding something back. It was as if there was something he wanted to say. But the moment passed as he pushed his hand through his dark blond hair and asked how her ice cream was.

Once finished, they made their way back to the car. As Lisa was about to get in, Nathan pulled her to him and kissed her. Lisa squealed at the unexpected gesture before relaxing in to the thoroughly lovely kiss that was an added sensation against the backdrop of the waterfall. When breathing became necessary, they broke apart.

'Wow! What was that for?'

Nathan grinned a wicked grin. 'I just wanted to kiss you in the Cascade du Rouget area.'

Giggling, Lisa got in the car. Instead of taking the road back down the mountain, they drove upward. Beyond the café the road continued to twist higher. They passed small farmsteads, where the only fence between them and the cows seemed to be white tape. Lisa kept her window open, the air helped with the post-ice-cream twisty-road sensation in her stomach, but also meant she could hear the cow bells. She didn't look down. The car seemed frequently too close to the rough edge of the too-narrow road and the sheer drop that threatened to give them a shortcut down the mountain.

When they reached the top, it was eminently worth it. The view across the ice-capped mountaintops was breath-taking. Nathan took a picnic basket and blanket from the boot of the car.

'When did you get those ready?'

'I had to do something to entertain myself when Flick and her tribe invaded our room.'

Nathan spread the blanket on the grass, near the shade of a tree.

'If I get down there, you might have to call search and rescue to haul me up.' Lisa grimaced.

'Yeah, I didn't think that part through!' Nathan laughed and looked around. 'How about that picnic bench?'

Lisa didn't want to seem ungrateful when Nathan had gone to the trouble of packing the blanket, but knew she would almost certainly get a numb bum on the ground. 'Do you mind?'

'Of course not.' Nathan shook the blanket off and carried the basket to the table.

They had a drink and admired the view before Nathan began unpacking the picnic. It looked perfect. Nathan had thought of all Lisa's favourites – even Maltesers and the white chocolate marshmallow bears she had discovered in the supermarché and grown a little too fond of were put on the table. Once everything was laid out, Nathan put his hand back inside the basket.

'Wait, there's something else.'

Lisa noticed his Adam's apple slide as he swallowed and the slight clench of his jaw.

'What is it?'

With an apprehensive smile, he took out the last of the items from the basket. It took Lisa a moment to realise that he was holding a ring box. It was black with a velvet covering. Tears welled in her eyes. Her heart thudded in her chest and she was pleased she was sitting down.

All of the tension gone from his face, Nathan smiled, knelt on one knee before her, and opened the box. The beautiful solitaire diamond on a gold band glinted a rainbow of colours in the sunshine. 'Lisa, will you marry me?'

The sight of Nathan on one knee, at what looked like the top of the world as blue sky, mountain peaks and tall pines stretched out before her, was overwhelming. It was more beautiful than she could ever have imagined. And it was just the two of them. Personal, intimate and perfect. The baby kicked as if to jolt her in to not keeping its daddy waiting. Lisa replied on a sob, 'Yes! Yes!'

Standing, Nathan slid the ring as far as he could onto her finger.

Almost perfect. 'Oh, my fingers are swollen with the heat.' Lisa couldn't believe it.

Nathan stopped trying to push the ring further on and smiled. 'That will do!'

Lisa stood as he swept her into a hug and they both cried happy tears.

Chapter Twenty-Four

The evening was spent celebrating and showing off the ring that thankfully fitted once Lisa was out of the heat of the sun and on lower ground. While Nathan called his parents, Lisa FaceTimed hers, and her brother, Luke – who was in Ireland but would soon be joining them in England. Felicity had been so happy for them Lisa had been concerned her screech of excitement would cause even the most resilient snow caps on the surrounding mountains to avalanche. Without hesitation Lisa had asked Felicity and her girls to be bridesmaids and Callum and Fred to be page boys, but told them there would be no wedding until the baby was born and she could fit in to something other than maternity clothes.

With the children in bed, and Flick and Pete sorting some bits of packing to give them a head start the following morning, the chalet was falling silent on their final evening. Lisa stood on the edge of the terrace, looking across the valley as lights began to shine in the chalets all around. Dom and Florian were at the end of the garden standing close, chatting. From the distance their stance looked intimate.

'Have you enjoyed your day?' Nathan put his arms round her, onto her bump.

'It's been perfect, really perfect. Do you think Dom will be OK when it's time to leave Florian?'

'I think he'll be fine. Besides, it turns out Florian's mum is English and so he has family in Brighton. As he mentioned he was overdue a trip to see them, and he does painting and decorating to pay the bills, I suggested he could combine the two. Come to England for a while and help finish the renovations on my place, while he's there. Make it fit for you and this one.' Nathan motioned to the baby.

'Really?' Lisa turned to Nathan. 'Does Dom know?'

'Of course. I wouldn't have suggested it without him agreeing first.'

Lisa hoped her excitement for Dom masked the fact that while she and Nathan had agreed, in a moment of post-engagement euphoria, that she should move into his place before the baby was born, she was less keen on doing so while Sam was still there.

Catching a glimpse of Lisa's ring in the moonlight, Nathan lifted her hand. 'I'm glad it fits.'

'So am I. I love it.'

'To be honest, I had thought about using the first one I got for you.'

'You kept it?' Lisa had no idea why she said that.

'Yes. Well, that is, I did … I definitely still had it when you first moved back to your parents'. I spent a whole evening looking at it after I got your friend request on Facebook.'

'You did?' Lisa remembered her drunken friend request, or at least the confirmation that Nathan had accepted it the following morning.

'But when I went to look at the ring recently, I couldn't find it. Can you believe that, after having it for eleven years?'

'I've got it.' Lisa bit her lip. Why did she say that? It sounded as if she had taken it, which she had, but not from him.

'What? … Why?' Nathan stepped back, confusion on his face.

'I found it.' *Found it!* Wishing she hadn't led herself down the path of having to explain 'finding it', she turned and sat down on the top step of the terrace.

'Lisa, it's OK. It was yours anyway. I just wondered why you'd take it and not say anything.' Nathan rubbed his forehead as he sat next to her, taking her hand in his.

Lisa swallowed to encourage saliva into her too-dry mouth. She remembered Nathan's words of earlier in the day and knew she should just speak to him – trust in him. 'It was in Sam's flat.'

'What? When? I mean … how?'

'The day I flew here I came looking for you. I could hear your phone in Sam's flat. I thought you might be there, so I went in. I wasn't snooping or anything.' *I was definitely snooping*.

'I was looking after Alex. We played tennis while Sam was out.'

So not there to see Sam. Not with Sam. The confirmation pleased her more than she expected. 'When I went to leave, I knocked Sam's bag over. The ring was on the floor. I don't know if it was in her bag or if it had been there under the sofa the whole time.'

'It must have been under the sofa, I don't know how, but maybe I dropped it there when I was sorting the flat.'

'Did you carry it around with you?'

'No. But it's the only logical explanation.'

I can definitely think of at least one more logical explanation.

'She'd have no reason for having it in her bag. You didn't think I'd given it to her, did you?' Nathan laughed, his expression incredulous.

Lisa didn't know if it was anger at herself for having let that exact thought enter her mind or Nathan's too-casual dismissal of Sam having the ring that was making her feel cross; either way she was aware her voice was too shrill as she spoke. 'She fancies you, you know. She could have taken it.'

'She doesn't fancy me. Her interest in me is purely as Alex's—'

'She does. She takes every opportunity to let me know. If you can't see it, you're blind or stupid.' Lisa couldn't believe her tone. After her beautiful day she was now sounding petulant.

'Honestly, Lisa, she doesn't fancy me. Not now.'

'So you admit she did.' Lisa looked into Nathan's eyes, searching for answers.

Raised tones meant Dom and Florian had made themselves scarce.

'Yes. But that was a long time ago, when we were teenagers. Soon after you left. She was a couple of years below us at school. I went with Brett to her sixteenth birthday party. He thought it would cheer me up. It didn't. I was feeling miserable and went upstairs; she cornered me, wanting … a birthday present, I guess.'

Lisa felt jealous at the thought of Sam alone with Nathan – her Nathan of all those years ago. She gripped his hand more tightly. *He's here now, with you.*

'Anyway, I left. She and Brett got together and have been together since.'

'Sam and Brett! Why didn't you just tell me that?'

'At first I didn't say because I thought it would be a surprise for you to see Brett once he came to join them, and then—'

'Alex is Brett's! I knew he looked familiar.' Lisa thought about the day she had seen him on the green with Sam; his smile was just as she remembered Nathan's friend Brett's at school. *She's Samantha Austin.* Lisa recalled Sam's name on her driving licence as it fell from her bag. *So they're married.* 'But it makes no sense.' Lisa wondered if she had seen pictures of Sam on Brett's Facebook page, but she had been intently looking for Nathan the night she searched his page and more than a little drunk. 'I knew Brett at school too. Why didn't you just tell me?'

'It's stupid, I know. But Sam was half-naked in my flat ... you didn't recognise her, and seeing you both together, I felt ... guilty, I guess.'

'Guilty? Why? You said nothing happened.' Lisa realised she had no right to sound accusing. She had left Nathan, after all. What he did during the time they were apart was not her business. She looked across the darkening valley. People in their chalets were going about their business; no matter what was occurring in the world, people's lives moved on.

'She kissed me and wanted to go further ... but I wasn't ready. She didn't taste like you. She didn't smell like you. I hated her for not being you, but more than anything I hated myself for losing you. Brett doesn't know what happened.'

Lisa didn't speak. She sat, taking in Nathan's words, holding his hand.

'When she was pregnant, she told me she had wanted the baby to be mine. How messed up is that? I couldn't tell Brett; he was happy.' Nathan laughed an empty laugh. 'He wanted me to be his best man, and then Alex's godparent. I couldn't say no. How could I have explained that?'

'Alex's godparent?'

'Yes.'

'She said you delivered him, is that right?'

Nathan laughed. 'I think you've misheard. I was there. I drove them. Brett had been drinking. And if sitting in the hospital canteen counts as being at the delivery I was there, but actually delivering Alex. No. I don't even want to imagine that.' Nathan mock shuddered.

Lisa hadn't realised how much that thought had been

bothering her, nagging at the back of her mind; hearing Nathan deny it, caused relief to flood through her and a breath to escape her. Lisa took a moment to absorb what he had said. The fact she knew she hadn't misheard Sam's words made her more sceptical about her actions. 'And does Sam love Brett at all?' At school Lisa hadn't been his biggest fan, but she didn't like to think of him in a one-sided or loveless relationship. Nobody deserved that.

'Yes, they're happy together, most of the time. Brett's job takes him round the world, so they move about and that can be tough. But the two of them are well-suited, and Alex is a good kid.'

'And where's Brett now?'

'Now? He's at my place with them. He's been doing a deal in Manchester. Sam and Alex wanted to stay down south and catch up with her family, so Brett asked if I could put them up for a bit. I told you I was letting the flat to an old friend, it was supposed to be a clue.'

'And that old friend was Brett, not Sam?'

'Yes. And letting isn't really the right word. They're just staying with me for a while. I think they'll be off again soon – maybe in the next couple of weeks.'

'Really?' Lisa tried not to sound too pleased at the news. Brett was Nathan's friend, and Alex was ... well, his godson, but, despite what Nathan thought, she couldn't help feel that Sam still had feelings for him. And with all that she had said about being in Nathan's flat, Lisa couldn't help but wonder if Sam had taken the ring.

Nathan looked at Lisa, his eyes dark in the moonlight. 'So, fiancée, shall we sit here talking about this, or shall we go to bed and celebrate our engagement?'

Lisa smiled at the word *fiancée* and raised an eyebrow at the suggestion. What was the point of talking about things that had happened so long ago, especially when it was her thirtieth birthday and her engagement day? The past was behind them, their future was growing healthily inside her, and the here-and-now was charged with desire and full of the promise evident in Nathan's wickedly enticing smile.

'Hmm, well, perhaps as I've technically got two engagement rings, we should celebrate twice.' She giggled.

Nathan stood before her and put out his hand. Lisa welcomed being pulled to her feet.

'Besides, that step was really giving me a numb bum!'

Chapter Twenty-Five

'Oh my goodness, Nathan, this is perfect!' Lisa took in the sight of the transformation the most recent renovations had made. Since returning from France, just over a month ago, she had spent less time staying at Nathan's place while work on converting the lower levels from the separate flats Nathan had almost completed, into a single dwelling took place. Nathan had pulled in favours from friends, and even the members of his watch had helped out where needed. The hallway had been opened up. The ground floor now consisted of a cloakroom with toilet, and a dayroom – leading through an archway to a kitchen-diner, with patio doors onto the currently still-overgrown garden that Pete was due to landscape for them. Original Edwardian features, such as the ornate tiles, fireplaces, ceiling roses and picture rails had been kept while the clean lines and open-plan living gave a modern feel. Lisa's eyes boggled as she attempted to take it all in. The rooms were light, bright and airy in the June sunshine.

'Do you like it?' Nathan looked at Lisa, his expression unsure.

'It's wonderful. As flats the building was impressive, but now … wow!'

Nathan grinned with relief, Lisa's approval making him more eager to show her the rest.

On the first floor, there was a further toilet and more formal lounge with views of the sea.

'I thought this would be cosier in the evening. But I guess we'll work it all out, once we start to live in it.'

Once we start to live in it. Lisa could hardly believe that the coming months would see her not only becoming a mum but also living with Nathan, in the beautiful home he had worked so hard to make for them. 'Of course.'

The second floor consisted of a double bedroom with en-suite and a nursery. Lisa and Nathan had purchased much of the equipment they would need for the baby but still had to finish decorating and to put it all in place. Lisa couldn't wait to unpack everything. Felicity had generously bought a baby bath full of "essentials" for them – some of which Lisa wasn't entirely sure she knew the purpose of, but hoped to have time to read up on before the baby arrived. She'd also received some gifts for the baby from clients; including a fleece blanket from Toby the Newfoundland's owner that she was pretty sure was meant for a dog.

The third floor remained as the flat Sam, Alex and now Brett shared, but plans were afoot to remove the kitchen area and to create two bedrooms with en-suite bathrooms, starting as soon as they moved out.

Lisa was pleased there was no hurry to alter the top floor; it held special memories of rediscovering Nathan and rebuilding their relationship. They could merely reassign the use of the rooms once they were using the lower levels as their main living area. Nathan wanted to set up some gym equipment. His job meant he had to keep fit and, while Felicity and Melissa had teased Lisa that being able to ogle Nathan doing a workout was a bit *Fifty Shades*, she had no objections to that prospect.

She and Nathan had also spoken about setting up an office area where she and Flick could have a desk and a whiteboard from which to coordinate their pet-sitting. With two – or two-and-a-half if you counted Fred – of them on the job, their reputation of offering one-to-one care and friendly, reliable service was growing. Recommendations meant business was booming. Lisa was also keeping up her magazine work and having somewhere to store the items sent for review would be beneficial. While some, such as the lead, had a quick turnaround, others took longer to test out – either due to the nature of the product, or her ability to use the item correctly and test it fairly. *Who knew a rabbit harness could be so difficult to put on?* Despite his owners giving permission, Doc McFluffins had been less compliant about the whole situation.

Aware Lisa was lost for words as she took everything in, Nathan spoke, 'Once Florian's finished painting the rooms he's agreed to do a mural in the nursery. You just need to decide what you want him to paint.'

'Wow! Really? That would be amazing.' An image slipped into Lisa's mind. She knew what she wanted, and just needed to speak to Florian before divulging it to Nathan.

'Yes, but I've given him strict instructions that your mum can't help.'

Lisa giggled as they made their way up the stairs. Her mum's painting had significantly improved under Florian's one-to-one tuition but remained a little abstract.

'How's he finding staying at your parents' place?' Nathan held the door open for Lisa.

Uno came to greet them, miaowing.

'Good, but he says between Mum's cooking and Winnie's biscuits, he's putting on weight.' Lisa crouched to stroke the cat as Nathan slipped his trainers off.

'So Florian has the Winnie seal of approval?' Nathan had met Winnie when Lisa took him round for a cup of tea. It had taken her a while and a lecture on never hurting Lisa before she offered him a biscuit, but once she had, he felt more than welcome.

'Well, she's added palmiers to the custard creams and

ginger nuts in the barrel. I'd say she's got them married off in her mind.'

'Palm what?'

'Palmiers – French biscuits.'

'Wow, he must have made a good impression.'

'Of course, he has. He's adorable.'

'Adorable?' Nathan raised an eyebrow, looking at Lisa bemused as they made their way to the kitchen.

'You know – charming, sweet but with an obvious intelligence behind his eyes.'

'Really?' Nathan scoffed, propping himself against the doorframe while Lisa got Uno's bowl.

'Yes, not my type at all.'

'Ha! Thanks for that.' Nathan laughed.

Lisa shook the cat's kibble into the bowl and placed it on the floor. Uno crouched into a ready to eat mode and began crunching. Lisa put the box of kibble away and smiled. 'You know my type.'

'Do I?'

'Yes … it's you.'

Nathan smiled, and Lisa kissed him. As she stepped back, she looked into his eyes. 'Thank you, by the way.'

'What for?'

'Offering Florian the work. Encouraging him to come over. This past month has given him and Dom a proper chance to get to know each other, they might really have something.'

'I had an ulterior motive.' A smile tugged at Nathan's lips.

Lisa looked at him, her expression serious. 'I told you Dom's just a friend, you don't need to play matchmaker—'

'Cheap labour,' he blurted the words with a laugh.

Lisa gasped before looking at Nathan's teasing expression. 'Oh, you're terrible.'

'Not really! I just wanted Dom to be happy, so you'd be happy. I saw how excited you were each time they went out together or stayed late on the terrace.'

'Well, that's really kind. Thank you.' Lisa leaned into Nathan's arms, the realisation dawning that her own efforts with his friends hadn't been nearly so generous. The "couple of weeks" Brett, Sam and Alex had intended to stay after Nathan and Lisa returned from France had stretched to four, and still, Lisa hadn't entirely warmed to the Austins.

Brett was fine; he and Lisa reminisced a little but primarily stuck to the safe subject of the renovations he had been lending a hand with. Finding Sam more pleasant in the company of others, Lisa had avoided being alone with her. She had attempted to get to know Alex better. But despite being similar in age to Flick's girls, he wasn't happy to chat about his interests like Megan; and he wasn't quirky like Alice. After a couple of failed attempts, Lisa had given up – perhaps too quickly. With their flights booked for the following evening and their departure set, Lisa knew she had one final evening to make amends. Brett and Sam were Nathan's friends after all, and their connection to Nathan meant they would be a part of her future. A farewell meal together would be a good way to say thank you for Brett's help and, Lisa hoped, a way to thaw some of the frost in her relationship with Sam.

Brett dominated the conversation talking about work throughout the meal. Lisa had to admire the fact having Alex had inspired him to take his higher education seriously. He'd applied himself as he never had at school, and had subsequently worked up to a job as a chief buyer for a large retailer. In the relaxed, slightly-alcohol-fuelled atmosphere he and Sam seemed happy, and Lisa was pleased. Alex had even smiled more times than she had seen him muster over the previous weeks, clearly enjoying his dad's stories.

Being almost thirty weeks pregnant, Lisa found it increasingly hard to finish a meal. She felt too full to manage all of the spaghetti bolognese she had served herself, and yet still she felt the familiar sting at the back of her throat and tightening in her chest of heartburn. Excusing herself, Lisa went to the kitchen and poured a glass of milk. The midwife had recommended a heartburn remedy but, even with the midwife's blessing and Flick's insistence she had lived on the stuff, Lisa didn't like to take medication while pregnant. The cold milk slipped down her throat easing the sensation a little. Lisa rubbed her hand over her hard bump. Winnie had told her heartburn was a sign the baby had lots of hair. Lisa had no idea if that was true.

As she placed the milk back in the fridge, Lisa glanced around the kitchen. She had removed her jewellery, putting it in a dish on the kitchen side, while she prepared the bolognese. Once finished Lisa had washed her hands and slipped her engagement ring on, deciding to leave her bracelet until after her shower. But she hadn't put it on, had she? Lisa put her hand to her empty wrist. No. She remembered Brett, Sam and Alex turning up before she'd had the opportunity. She had gone into hostess mode, wanting everything to be perfect. But if she hadn't put it on and the dish she was staring at was now empty, where was it? Her thoughts flicked to Sam. Had she had the opportunity to take it? Lisa remained almost certain she had taken and secreted away the engagement ring Nathan had kept from their prom. But she hadn't confronted Sam about it. How could she without revealing how she discovered it?

But now her bracelet was missing. Lisa thought about the charms on it – the fireman, Uno, the satchel and, of course, her pip. Not knowing where it was caused the tightness in her chest to increase. Nathan appeared at the kitchen door.

'You OK?'

Lisa wondered whether to say about the bracelet and her suspicions.

'Thanks for tonight. I know Brett's never been your favourite person, and that things got off on the wrong foot with Sam, but this has been nice; a new beginning. I really appreciate it.'

And just like that Lisa knew she couldn't say what was on her mind. She felt desperate about her bracelet, and she was certain Sam had something to do with its disappearance, but she couldn't bring herself to hurt Nathan. Her reasons for accusing Sam couldn't be shared in front of Brett and Alex. Not when the repercussions could result in Nathan losing his best friend and his godson.

Lisa took a steadying breath and welcomed a hug from Nathan. Knowing he would agree that she should lay down she told him she felt suddenly tired. It was an easy way out of a situation in which she was unsure she could hold back from blurting out what she wanted to say. But with Sam's departure imminent she knew she would have to do something to discover the truth, and she would have to do it soon.

Chapter Twenty-Six

Felicity moved the driftwood lamp and looked behind it. She, Lisa and Fred had been searching Nathan's flat for over an hour.

Lisa looked at her. 'I told you, it was in the dish on the kitchen side. It would hardly have got up and walked into the living room.'

'No. I agree, but you can't accuse anyone of taking it before you have searched everywhere. What if Nathan moved it?'

Lisa had called Felicity as soon as Nathan had left for work, telling her about her missing bracelet and confiding her suspicions.

'I asked him if he'd seen it when he came to bed last night.'

'And?' Felicity moved the cushions on the sofa for the second time, while Fred crawled around the floor, searching for the missing "treasure".

Lisa sighed. 'He kissed me, made a joke about my baby brain and said it couldn't be far. Then he fell asleep.'

'Typical! OK, so Nathan didn't move it. What about Uno?'

'Uno? Flick he's a cat, not a bloody magpie.'

Fred giggled.

'I know that. But the bracelet has dangly things on it, cats like dangly things.'

Lisa pointed to Uno, snoozing on the cat bridge. 'He spent most of the evening up there. I'm pretty sure I would have noticed if he'd started running around with my bracelet.'

'OK.' Felicity looked at Lisa's sullen face. 'I know you're

upset. And if what you've told me about the engagement ring is true – and I don't know why you failed to mention that until today – then Sam possibly has form, but Lisa,' Felicity put her arm around Lisa's shoulder, 'we have to be sure. Imagine Brett finding out about Sam's feelings for Nathan now.'

A side table falling to the ground as Fred attempted to crawl under it caused them both to look in his direction.

'Oh poo bags!' Fred stood up, his face looking innocent.

'Fred! Don't say that,' Felicity admonished.

'Fred, you're a genius!' Lisa began searching her pockets for her phone.

Fred looked between his mum and Lisa, clearly preferring Lisa's assessment of the situation he gave her a smile.

Felicity looked at Lisa dumbfounded.

'The Pet Cam!'

The Pet Cam lay on the floor amongst the letters and books Nathan had left on the table.

Felicity crouched to pick the items up, while Lisa hurried to get her phone having remembered it was on charge in the kitchen.

Felicity called after her, 'Setting it up now won't do you any good. Didn't you say they're leaving tonight?' Felicity stood up and looked as if she'd just had an idea. 'Unless we bait Sam.' She gasped. 'I think Alice has a fingerprinting kit.'

Lisa returned to the room. 'Flick, we're not Cagney and Lacey! We're not going to bait anyone, and we won't need a fingerprinting kit. Hopefully, we'll have all the evidence we need right here.'

'But I thought you couldn't set it up?'

'I couldn't, but then I watched a YouTube tutorial and got it sorted – did you know they have tutorials for everything on YouTube? Literally everything.'

'Really? I hardly use it. The children do though.' Felicity grimaced, before shaking her head and returning to the point. 'So you got the Pet Cam set-up—'

'And there wasn't really anything to report. Though it did confirm Uno loves the cat bridge; he sleeps a lot!'

'So how will the Pet Cam help us now? Do you think it might have been Uno after all?'

'No,' Lisa scoffed. 'But the camera faces Uno's bridge and the doorway to the kitchen, we'll see who went in there and—'

'I've found it!' Fred beamed as he shouted excitedly holding aloft the treasure he had discovered down the back of the sofa.

Lisa's heart leapt. She would happily be proven wrong about Sam if it meant she got her bracelet back. As she took in the sight of the pound coin Fred held in his dimpled hand she tried not to let her disappointment show. 'That's great Fred. You can keep it.' She attempted to smile before returning her attention to her phone.

Felicity rubbed Lisa's arm apologetically. 'Hey, Fred I've got an idea.' Felicity went to her bag and took out a notebook and a pack of twistable crayons. 'You should draw a map, to show us where you found it?'

Felicity guided Fred to the table, ensuring he was fully engaged in the activity before returning to Lisa, who was staring at her phone.

'The Pet Cam's movement activated, you can scroll up to four hours of recording via the app. It might show something.'

'But don't you turn it off when you come in?'

'I'm supposed to, but to be honest, until Fred knocked it off the table, I'd forgotten about it. The novelty of checking it wore off after a couple of days. It's probably more appropriate for kittens, like Kit and Kaboodle ... Look there's footage!'

'That's us, this morning. Ha! There's me with my cup of tea.' Felicity giggled.

'Good, so we know it's working. We just need to hope there haven't been more than four hours of activity since my bracelet was taken.' Lisa scrolled through the footage.

She and Felicity leaned forward staring at the phone screen.

'Look, that's me after my shower last night, I'm in my towel.'

'There's Nathan.'

'Oh!' Lisa's cheeks flushed as she hurriedly forwarded through the recording.

'Wait! What was going on there?'

'Nothing,' Lisa squeaked, her cheeks burning hotter while she made a mental note to check if recordings were stored for any period on the device itself.

'Right, look food leaving the kitchen. The Austins have arrived.'

'OK.'

They watched as Lisa and Nathan went in and out of the kitchen, and Uno stretched as he moved positions.

'Look, there's Sam!' Felicity pointed at the screen. 'That's a short skirt. Her legs are so—'

'Flick, that's not helping.'

'Sorry, it's just—'

'I know!'

'OK. So she's gone straight past the kitchen door—'

'To the toilet, and back again,' Lisa finished.

Felicity looked at Lisa. 'And you definitely didn't leave the bracelet in the bathroom?'

Lisa sat back from her phone. 'No. I remember leaving it

in the kitchen.' She swallowed past the lump in her throat. 'I really did.' She pictured it exactly where she left it and felt tears sting her eyes. 'Honestly, Flick, my brain hasn't entirely turned to mush, I know where I left my bracelet!'

Felicity put her hand on Lisa's arm. 'We'll get to the bottom of it. Pass your phone. I'll look while you grab yourself a tissue.'

Lisa passed Felicity her phone, stepped over her feet and went to the kitchen. As she wiped her face, she took a breath. She just wanted her bracelet back. Proving that Sam wasn't as innocent as Nathan believed she was would be a bonus, but more than anything she wanted her bracelet back where it belonged. Nathan had given it to her to fill with memories. How could she do that if it were lost? Fresh tears threatened to run down her cheeks.

'Lisa quick!'

Lisa dashed to the lounge. 'What is it?'

Felicity looked at her, eyes wide, holding the phone, the recording paused. 'Here's your culprit. Caught red-handed!'

Lisa looked from the screen back to Felicity. Attempting to take the revelation in, she swallowed.

Chapter Twenty-Seven

Having convinced Felicity she should do this alone and that she certainly didn't want to wait for Nathan to return from his shift, Lisa found herself sitting on the very sofa she had discovered her engagement ring under, facing Sam. Why hadn't she taken longer to consider what to say? While Sam looked at her expectantly, Lisa stumbled over her words. Thank goodness Brett was out. She was sure having him there too wouldn't make it any easier. As it was, Alex was in the kitchen, within earshot. The whole situation had the potential to go very wrong, but at least she had the screenshot. The evidence on her phone, held in her hand, gave her a momentary boost of confidence. She took a breath.

'The thing is, last night, when you came upstairs, something, something of mine ...'

Lisa heard Alex still in the kitchen.

'Something of mine went missing.'

Sam, looked at her affronted, her normal soft, full lips hardened. 'And?'

'And I know who took it.'

Sam sat forward, folding her arms on her knees, her eyes meeting Lisa's in an unflinching stare. 'So why are you here? You're not seriously suggesting one of us—'

'No. I'm not suggesting it was one of you. I know it was one of you.'

Sam let out a breath, before standing. 'What the...? Does Nate know you're here?'

Lisa decided to remain seated, it was less confrontational and proved she was going to stay and have her say. Her heart was beating too fast, and her foot had developed an uncontrollable shake, but she was determined not to leave until she had her bracelet and an explanation.

'No. I thought it might be better to keep this between us, for now.'

'For now? What does that mean?'

It means if I don't get what I've come for, I'll be calling Nathan for reinforcements. 'It means I'm giving Alex a chance to explain and to return my bracelet.'

A clatter sounded from the kitchen as crockery was dropped onto the floor. Sam and Lisa both jumped.

'Are you mad?' Sam glared at Lisa.

Alex appeared from the kitchen door, his face ashen.

Sam motioned for him to stay where he was before turning back to Lisa. 'How dare you accuse my son? You'd better get out.' Her voice was thick with anger.

Lisa sat still, her eyes fixed on Alex, ignoring Sam. *Don't leave. Get what you came for.* 'I'm not cross, but I do want it back.'

'What are you saying? I'm calling Nate.' Sam picked up her bag, shoving her hand in as she scrabbled for her phone.

Lisa lifted her gaze to Alex. 'Do you want him to know? I haven't told him.'

'Mum, wait!' Alex moved to Sam, placing his hand over her phone.

'What? Why?' Sam looked between Alex and Lisa confusion in her eyes while anger remained evident in the clench of her jaw and the grip she had on her phone.

'Why don't we all sit down?' Lisa amazed herself by sounding calmer and more collected than she actually felt. Inside she was trembling. The boy's face, his caught-in-the-headlights expression and the quiver in his hand, made her wish she had spoken to him alone. Lisa didn't know why he had taken the bracelet, or if he had taken the ring and she wished she'd given him the chance to explain before putting him in the firing line of a now angry Sam.

Alex sat at the opposite end of the sofa to Lisa, his head bowed, while Sam perched on the edge of the table, not committing to actually sitting. With the silence in the room adding to the weight of the anger-fuelled atmosphere, Lisa decided to speak.

'Last night my bracelet, the one Nathan got me, went missing. I wasn't sure where I put it, baby brain I guess, so I checked Uno's Pet Cam.' Lisa was aware she was sugar-coating the truth, but '*I was pretty sure you'd taken it Sam and decided to search for proof*' definitely wouldn't have helped an already tense situation.

'Pet Cam?' Sam questioned.

'A camera that's directed where Uno sleeps. It takes in the hallway and the door to the kitchen too. I meant to turn it off, but I forgot.'

'Like you forgot where you put your bracelet.' Sam's words were laced with sarcasm.

Lisa coughed. 'Yes.' *No, I know exactly where I left my bracelet*. She was aware Sam was trying to discredit anything she had to say. She continued, 'the camera is motion activated so as we were going in and out of the kitchen last night it was recording us.'

'Spying on us,' Sam interjected, making herself appear the injured party.

Alex shifted uneasily in his seat.

'No. If it hadn't have been for trying to find my bracelet I would never have even looked at the recording.'

'So you looked. What did you see?' Sam folded her arms, waiting for Lisa's response.

Lisa swallowed.

'Me ... taking the bracelet,' Alex's voice came out as an uneven whisper.

Sam looked at Alex taken aback, while Lisa nodded silently.

'What?' Sam's cheeks flushed as she looked at Alex, and then at Lisa. Her reaction confirmed she had no idea Alex had taken the bracelet, or what to say next.

'Do you still have it?' *Please say yes.* Lisa hadn't thought that he might have discarded it, until now.

Tears formed in Alex's eyes as he nodded.

'But, why? Why would you do that?' Sam turned from Alex to Lisa. 'He's never taken anything before.'

Lisa thought about the engagement ring and wondered if that was true.

Alex took a shaky breath. 'I saw it in the kitchen. It's got Nate and Uno on it.'

'Yes, Nate showed us. You remember how happy he was when he bought it for her?'

Knowing Nathan had shown her bracelet to Sam and Alex stung a little, but Lisa welcomed the fact Sam acknowledged it made him happy to get it for her.

Alex nodded.

'Then why would you do this, after all he's done for us? How do you think Nate will feel about you taking it?' Some of the anger had gone from Sam's tone. As confusion took over, she looked at Alex questioningly.

Lisa was surprised. She had seen Sam as an enemy over the previous months, not truly recognising her role as Alex's mum and Nathan's friend.

'Sad. Angry,' Alex mumbled.

'I don't think he'd be angry,' Lisa interjected. 'Though he might want to know why?'

Sam looked gratefully at Lisa before turning her attention back to Alex. The boy bit his bottom lip. Lisa wondered if it might bleed as his teeth sunk in turning the pressure points white.

'I would like to know why, too,' Sam added.

Alex sniffed. He looked at Lisa. 'Because she's taking Nate away from us. He won't have time for us when she lives here with the baby.' Alex pointed an accusing finger at Lisa's bump. 'She already made him change the house, and we won't be able to stay any more.'

'Alex, you know Nate will always have time for you. He loves you.' Sam put her hand on the boy's leg.

Lisa didn't know what to say. She had spent weeks thinking that Sam wanted to infiltrate her relationship with Nathan and hadn't stopped to consider the impact her presence might be having on the relationship he already had with Sam and Alex. Had she pushed them out? Should she have tried harder to get to know them properly? Lisa thought about the day she had returned to find a semi-naked Sam in Nathan's flat. On that day at least, Sam had intended to make her feel uncomfortable, of that she was sure.

'But it won't be the same.' A single tear spilt from Alex's eye.

Sam slipped her hand around the boy's shoulder. 'No because things change, and people change.' She looked at Lisa. 'But change can be a good thing. There'll be a new baby, but you can teach it the things Nate has taught you, like how to surf – when it's older.'

'And there'll always be a place here for you to stay, not in a separate flat but in the house. We'll have spare rooms,' Lisa added. 'Nathan would be sad if you couldn't come to stay again. And I want him to be happy. Don't you?'

Alex wiped his hand across his face. 'Yes.'

'Then you'd better give Lisa her bracelet back.' Sam spoke calmly but decisively.

Alex slipped his hand in his pocket and pulled the bracelet out.

It was right there all the time. Lisa blinked away relief-fuelled tears as she took it. Her bracelet, with all the charms, including her precious pip, was back where it belonged – with her.

'And what do you say?' Sam asked.

'I'm sorry for taking your bracelet.' Alex looked at Lisa, his red-rimmed eyes bright against his pale skin.

'And …' Sam pressed.

Alex sniffed before speaking, 'And your engagement ring.'

'What?' Sam looked at Alex aghast. 'I meant you should say it won't happen again. Please tell me you haven't also taken Lisa's engagement ring!' Sam's eyes flicked to Lisa's hands.

Two hours later, Lisa sat with her feet up on the sofa with Uno snuggled next to her, and listened as Felicity reiterated what she had just told her over the telephone:

'So Alex took … the ring in the hope … Nathan wouldn't ask you to … marry him?'

'Yes, why are you so out of breath? Ewww, I haven't interrupted something have I?'

'No … I've just finished a run.'

'Phew! OK. Well, Nathan had shown him the ring once, when Alex had needed to borrow … oh, I can't remember, something sporty. Alex met me, remembered the ring and took it the next time he visited Nathan.'

'What did Sam say?'

'She was shocked and embarrassed about the whole thing. But she was also apologetic and not just for Alex's behaviour but her own. She realised the way she'd been treating me had contributed to Alex's actions.'

'Wow, she said that?'

Lisa gulped down the mouthful of squash she had just taken. 'Yes. After Alex had been sent to his room to await his punishment – I think it is going to involve his Xbox and a lot of spare time on his hands – we actually had a good talk. Sam explained she'd implied things that weren't true because she wanted to make me feel jealous. Not because she still has feelings for Nathan but because that's how she had felt when he rejected her, because of his feelings for me.'

'That's messed up.'

'Yes. But I think the fact I hadn't remembered her on that first day when her memories of me were raw in her mind brought out—'

'The bitch in her?'

'No. I was going to say her darker side.'

'OK, we'll go with that.'

Lisa stroked Uno's soft, warm fur. 'What she did, and what Alex did, it's strange behaviour, but it does prove they really care for Nathan.'

'I guess. I'm pleased you got it sorted. And will you tell Nathan?'

'No. If Sam had been the culprit, then, of course I would. But Alex knows he did the wrong thing. I've got my bracelet and the ring back. Things are better between all of us now we've spoken.' Lisa knew jealousy could make people behave out of character and hoped Alex would learn rash actions weren't a solution.

'That makes sense.'

'I thought so.' Lisa smiled to herself. It was the right decision. The grown-up decision.

'Lisa, you're going to keep the screenshot though aren't you? I mean there's no harm in keeping the evidence. Just in case.'

'Of course, I am. I'm forgiving, not a fool.'

Chapter Twenty-Eight

Lisa waved goodbye to Florian wishing him a lovely day out with Dom, before returning to the nursery. Florian had done a fantastic job. She was delighted with the mural, and after not letting Nathan see it as a work in progress she now couldn't wait to show him. Under Florian's tutorage, she had even let her mum do a little of it. It made it even more personal. It was mid-July and the baby was due in two weeks. Having officially moved into Nathan's – or their place as he insisted it now was – Lisa was finally feeling as if she would be ready by the time the baby arrived. Felicity had taken on more of her pet-sitting duties, but Lisa was still keeping her hand in. She couldn't let her favourite clients down and had an appointment booked in to walk Jack a little later in the day – an excuse for a catch-up with Winnie too.

Lisa wandered into the lounge and picked up her laptop. She and Felicity sometimes posted photographs to their Facebook page while pet-sitting or on dog walks. It kept the page active as clients enjoyed stopping by to see their pet's antics; an idea Lisa had got from the Pet Cam. Sure enough, Felicity had posted a picture of Doc McFluffins enjoying a cabbage leaf. Lisa smiled.

As she returned to her news feed, Lisa noticed an alert from the *Gazette* advising of an incident causing chaos on the local roads. The picture showed an ambulance and fire engines on the A27. She thought about Nathan and hoped there were no fatalities. He didn't always share the things he saw or dealt with at work, but Lisa was mindful of the fact there were times when he just needed her to be there, to listen to the highs and lows while he vented about his day. Scrolling through the *Gazette* page, she tried to read what had happened but couldn't follow the article as advertisements filled the screen.

Lisa closed her laptop and decided to text her mum to check she was OK. She knew she and her dad were due to pick up her brother from the airport and wanted to make sure they weren't involved in the incident. Confirmation soon came that they were too far on in their journey to be affected. Lisa was relieved, and excited to know she would soon see Luke. While Lisa had hoped he would return to England for Easter, the appeal of staying longer in Ireland with his girlfriend had won out. They had called and FaceTimed each other regularly but the fact he was now en route home meant she was guaranteed a proper catch-up with him before the baby arrived.

As she went to move from the sofa, Lisa felt her stomach tightening. She gritted her teeth waiting for the tension to pass. She had felt a few false contractions in the night, making her uncomfortable, and sleep difficult. Lisa hissed through her teeth as the pain lasted longer than she had previously experienced. When it eventually eased she felt relieved, and a little light-headed. Uno meowed at her, hungrily.

'OK, I'm coming.' Lisa slid herself to the edge of the sofa and stood up. She was feeling more cumbersome by the day. Her increasing size, combined with the summer heat meant she was often uncomfortable. The midwife had said she was carrying a big baby and she knew it. It frequently dug under her ribs and pushed down on her bladder as it fought for space. Sleeping had become difficult as she found it harder to get comfortable in bed, and switching positions had become akin to doing a five-point turn.

With Uno contentedly eating, Lisa decided to get ready for her appointment with Jack and Winnie. Halfway up the stairs, her stomach began to tighten once more, but this time the sensation was lower and intensified like a strong period pain. She clutched her stomach. *It's too early. There are two weeks to go.* While the pain continued, she had no choice but to stay still. When finally it eased, Lisa returned back downstairs to her phone. The Braxton Hicks she had previously experienced were not as strong as those she was feeling now. Lisa didn't want to make a fuss, but she also didn't want to leave it too late to call for help if labour had started.

Remembering from her antenatal classes that she was supposed to time her contractions to establish if there was a pattern to them, she turned her phone on. *Wait, do I time from the start or the end, when am I supposed to start and stop the clock?* As she went to Google it another pain gripped her. Forgetting all she'd learnt about breathing the pain away she growled. She didn't know how long it had been since the last contraction, but they seemed close. She didn't want to phone the fire station. Even if she could get a message to Nathan, the accident almost certainly meant the watch would be busy. For all she knew the contractions were a false alarm. Remembering that Florian said Dom was off work Lisa called him.

'Rose, Gran says you're walking Jack today so I might stop by before I meet Flor—'

'How will I know when I'm in labour?'

'What? Why? Do you think you're in labour?'

'No. Well maybe. I've been having false contractions. It's probably just more of them. There are still two weeks to go.'

'All right, but if you're not sure you should call the hospital and speak to the midwife.'

'I will. It's probably nothing. Braxton Hicks.'

'Are you timing them?'

About to ask exactly how to do that, Lisa felt another contraction coming on. 'Will do.' She hung up, and rode out the pain. This time it didn't last so long. *So they're irregular, I'm not in established labour.* Lisa had no idea where the thought came from or if it was correct, but it gave her some comfort. She had read so much on the subject, attended her antenatal classes and watched TV programmes – forwarding the parts that looked painful – believing she'd retained some knowledge gave her hope that everything would be all right. She tried to think, what else could she remember? Thoughts spun in her mind and panic began to set in. Unsure what she should be doing or if what she was experiencing was even the start of labour Lisa decided to call Felicity. *She'll know what to do.*

Lisa waited while the phone rang.

'Hello, Lisa? It said Lisa.' Callum's voice was squeaky and curious.

'Callum, it is me. Is Mummy there?'

'Yes.'

Relieved, Lisa blew out a breath and waited. And waited. 'Callum?'

'Yes?'

'Can I speak to Mummy?'

'No.'

Lisa could hear laughter in Callum's voice. 'Really? Why not? I'd really like to.'

'She's chasing the rabbit.'

'She's what?'

'Chasing the rabbit.' Callum giggled wildly. 'And it's really fast!'

Oh no! 'Do you mean Doc McFluffins?'

Lisa heard more wild giggles down the phone as a vision of Doc McFluffins running speedily around the garden with Felicity in hot pursuit entered her mind. 'Callum, Callum?'

'Yes?'

'Is Alice or Megan with you?'

'Yes.'

'Can I speak … please, can you pass Megan the phone?' Lisa could hear laughter and chaos ensuing in the background, before finally hearing the phone being passed over.

'Hello.'

'Megan, it's Lisa.'

'Mummy didn't mean to let the rabbit out, he bit her.' Megan's voice was defensive on her mum's behalf.

'Megan it's fine, he's a feisty rabbit. But I do need to speak to your mummy. Do you know how to switch to speakerphone?'

Lisa had no idea what the noise Megan made meant, but she guessed it was an indication that she had asked a stupid question.

'Done. Mummy, Lisa wants you, she's on speaker.'

Panting Felicity shouted, 'Sorry Lisa. I—'

'Flick I think the baby's coming.'

'What?'

Lisa felt pain grip her stomach once more. 'Oww, oww, oww,' her voice was a whimper.

Felicity spoke directly into the phone, 'Lisa, do you have contractions?'

Lisa couldn't answer.

'When you can I want you to phone the hospital. Is Nathan with you?'

'No … he's at work.'

'Right I'll be there as soon as I've caught Doc McFluffins.

Megan, Alice, Callum, Fred, stop laughing and help me get that rabbit back in his hutch. Lisa needs us. Her baby's coming.'

Lisa heard a squeal of excitement. With the pain easing off she was able to speak again. 'Thank you. Am I still on speaker phone?'

'No.'

'Flick, what if I just need a big poo?'

'Do you feel like you need a big poo?'

'Yes—'

'OK. Definitely, don't sit on the toilet. Phone the hospital. Put the front door on the latch, and we'll be with you soon. Don't push anything out until we get there!'

'Wait! What?'

Lisa ran the bath the midwife told her to take. Not Lisa's usual midwife, the lady at the end of the phone had advised that as this was Lisa's first delivery, it would be hours before the baby made an appearance. Lisa was relieved but equally scared. If there were hours to go how much more intense would the pain get? Between contractions, she felt normal but when they came, the pain was all-consuming. She'd contemplated calling the fire station but once again decided against it. If the incident was as bad as it looked on her phone, people needed Nathan more than she did, at least for the next few hours. *Please let the midwife be right about that.*

As Lisa went to lift Nathan's T-shirt over her head, she felt a pop in her groin. Warm liquid flooded down her legs. Lisa looked at it in horror, wondering if she had wet herself the way Melissa had described before realisation dawned. Her waters had broken. She threw a towel onto the floor in the hope of mopping it up. An intense pain surged low down in her pelvis. Lisa gripped the sink and growled. She had no idea where the sound was coming from – guttural, primitive, deeper than any noise she'd ever made before.

'Lisa! Lisa, we're here.'

Unable to speak or move, Lisa waited for the pain to pass – her knuckles white as she clung to the sink and rocked her hips. When it eased, she began to cry with relief, grateful that Felicity had arrived.

She heard Felicity call from the stairs, 'Dom's here too. I found him outside.'

'You didn't show up to walk Jack. After your call I was worried,' Dom explained.

Lisa grabbed a towel and wrapped it around her lower half. Pushing the sweat covered strands of hair that had escaped from her ponytail back from her face, she moved to the bathroom door.

Felicity and Dom were on the stairs, the children standing behind them, eyes wide. 'You sounded like a lion.' Fred sniggered as he and Callum began replicating the noise Lisa had been making just moments before.

Felicity turned to the children. 'Megan, will you take them and keep them downstairs? Put on the TV, feed them snacks, let them explore the garden, whatever it takes just keep them busy.' Returning her attention to Lisa, Flick continued. 'Have your waters broken?'

'Yes.'

'Have you called the hospital?'

'Yes, before. They told me to take a bath.'

'They always say that.' Felicity rolled her eyes. 'Have you called Nathan?'

'No, there's an accident, the *Gazette* said emergency services were attending.'

'A lorry's overturned on the A27, nobody's hurt, but the road is closed; everywhere's rammed,' Dom affirmed.

'Right well I'm calling Pete to see if he can get hold of Nathan. While I do that, why don't you let Dom come and see how you're getting on? You know, assess the state of play.' Felicity motioned to Lisa's bump.

'What? No.' Lisa pulled her towel tighter around herself.

Dom moved further up the stairs. 'Lisa I can help you. It's my job. This is what I do.'

'But you can't see my foof!'

'Let's just focus on making sure you and the baby are all right. You might have hours yet. And if it comes to it, I promise to clear your foof from my memory.'

'No. If you see my foof, it will change everything.'

Felicity looked between them. 'Why do you both keep saying foof?'

'They mean vagina!'

Felicity gasped and spun around. 'Good grief Alice, will you go and help Megan with your brothers.'

Alice stood, reluctant to remove herself from the action.

'I promise I'll call if we need you.'

Alice turned on her heels and went to find the others, her grin suggesting she welcomed the prospect of a responsibility not bestowed upon her siblings.

Lisa began to moan as another contraction took hold. Dom ran up the stairs to steady her. She gripped his hands as the pain started to intensify.

Felicity looked at Dom. 'Let's wait until this one passes and then move her to the bedroom.'

'I'm not sure she's going to make it to the hospital. The roads out of town are in chaos; I think we'd be mad to try. I'll call and speak to the delivery suite,' Dom affirmed.

Lisa growled more deeply.

'Judging by that noise, I'd say this baby wants to come out. So how about if I do the looking and you tell me what to do?' Felicity suggested.

'It's a plan. But seriously, I am happy to look.'

'Nooooooooooooo!' Lisa made her thoughts on the matter clear.

After an examination that revealed there wasn't time to make it to the hospital, and a call to the delivery suite resulting in the confirmation that they'd endeavour to get a midwife to them as soon as possible, Dom gave Felicity a list of items needed to assist with the birth. She looked at it, at first perplexed, then soon realised she knew just where to source certain essentials and decided to enlist Alice's help. At least the fact Lisa's hospital bags were packed meant bits for her and the baby were in one easy to find spot. The rest needed a little sourcing and imagination.

Hurrying upstairs with the most recent box of pet paraphernalia sent from *Paws About Town* magazine, followed by Alice carrying Lisa's bag of emergency supplies from her van Felicity grabbed towels from the airing cupboard before pausing at the bedroom door.

'Stay out here Alice.'

'Mummy, when I'm a doctor—'

Lisa growled from inside the room. Alice looked at Felicity. 'I'll leave this here.' She placed the bag on the floor.

Felicity registered the concern on her daughter's face and winked. 'You've been a big help. I'll tell Lisa, and I am sure she'll be really grateful.'

Alice grinned and walked back down the stairs, her head held high.

Felicity scooped up the bag handle and rushed into the

room, dropping the towels and emptying the box and bag. Labour wasn't the exact intention for a pet heat pad, a waterproof car boot liner, a "nighttime walkies" head torch, or the plastic bags, gloves, tissues and anti-bac essentials in Lisa's cat poo ninja kit, but they were all new and about to be put to good use.

Once Lisa was manoeuvred onto her layered bed of plastic sheets and towels, and Dom had teased about the head torch being a step too far, Felicity agreed to check on Lisa's progress. As Dom turned his back and Felicity went to look, Lisa moaned as another contraction began taking hold. She looked at Felicity and Dom, eyes wide, with the increasing intensity of pain she growled through gritted teeth, 'I want to push. Forget my foofing foof and get this baby ouuuuuuut!'

Slipping the towel back from Lisa's knees Felicity looked. 'Oh my goodness, it's coming, the head is crowning! I've never seen it all from this angle.'

Assessing the situation, Dom advised Lisa to pant.

'Thank goodness you're here.' Felicity smiled at Dom gratefully. Driving over she'd feared the traffic meant she might have to deliver Lisa's baby, with the assistance of her children and a YouTube tutorial.

Eventually, Lisa's contraction subsided. She took a moment of respite while Dom reassured her that it wouldn't be long until she was holding her baby.

As the bedroom door opened, Felicity and Dom turned in unison.

Dressed in his blues, Nathan stood in the doorway relief evident in his expression at having not missed the birth.

'You made it through the traffic.' Felicity beamed.

'It turns out Nathan's got connections.' Pete spoke before peering over Nathan's shoulder. 'Oh Christ, sorry!' Covering his eyes with his hand, he turned back to the stairs. 'I'll go and check on the children.'

Thanking Felicity and Dom for being there, Nathan went to Lisa's side. Clearly relieved at his arrival, she let out a sob, before grabbing his hand as another contraction started.

'OK, Nathan, do you want to deliver your baby?' Dom asked.

Nathan kissed Lisa's forehead. 'Yes.'

As the contraction intensified, Lisa cried out.

Felicity moved to take hold of her hand, freeing Nathan to move to the end of the bed. Dom stood to the side, advising what to do, while Nathan prepared to meet his and Lisa's baby.

Chapter Twenty-Nine

After a belated visit from the midwife, who had confirmed all was well with mother and baby, first Nathan's, and then Lisa's parents and brother arrived. Felicity served yet more tea. Following a round of cuddles for Lisa and the baby, and several reassurances that he hadn't seen anything he shouldn't, Pete had taken the children home with the promise they would all see the baby again soon. Upon Nathan's insistence, Dom had stayed to help finish the bottle of champagne Nathan had stowed away in readiness for the birth. Everybody wanted to offer their congratulations and to have their first cuddle with the new arrival. Lisa watched as her eight pound four ounce, precious bundle was passed from person to person. Having everyone there was wonderful, but also a little overwhelming.

While Lisa sat down taking in the events of the day, Nathan's mum brought her a glass of water. 'You'll need this, you have to keep your fluids up.'

'Thank you.' Lisa smiled.

Valerie perched on the arm of Lisa's seat. 'Lisa. I wanted to say how happy I am you came back and … well … thank you.'

'Thank you, for what?'

'For making Nathan the happiest I've ever seen him, and for making me the proudest grandparent alive.'

Lisa glanced at her own parents cooing over the baby and knew Valerie would have a fight on her hands for that title. Having got the words off her chest, Valerie went to move, but Lisa caught her arm. 'I meant to ask you. What did you mean when you said Uno rescued Nathan?' The question had remained in the back of Lisa's mind. There hadn't been a suitable time to ask but while Valerie was opening up seemed an appropriate opportunity.

Valerie turned and hesitated. 'I shouldn't have said it ... It was just so hard back then, Nathan was so hurt, and lost his direction for a while. But becoming a firefighter and then learning to love that cat made him whole again. Uno taught him it was OK to love, and how to smile again.'

Lisa felt an ache in her chest. She didn't know what to say.

Valerie placed her hand over Lisa's and patted it. 'It's in the past, Lisa. Look at him now. That little bundle means he'll always have a reason to be happy. You've given him that.'

Lisa caught Nathan's eye as he looked at her across the room; she welcomed the warm smile he gave her and the love she could see in his eyes.

When the doorbell rang, Felicity went to answer it while Dom looked at Lisa apologetically.

'I hope you don't mind. I can't drive home now I've had a drink, so I called Florian.'

'Of course I don't mind.'

'Only, he wasn't allowed to come alone.'

Lisa looked past Felicity to see Florian and Winnie, and welcomed them both with a big smile. Felicity made the introductions before fetching a plate for the custard creams Winnie had brought as a gift for Lisa.

'And this is for the little one.' With a big smile, Winnie passed Lisa a card and a soft package before taking a seat on the sofa – her feet barely reaching the floor.

Opening the card, Lisa was touched by the beautiful words Winnie had written and read them aloud: 'Congratulations my lovelies, and when the days feel long remember the years are all too short, treasure every moment with your precious baby!' As Lisa looked up to thank Winnie and reassure her that she intended to do exactly that, she noticed her mum, Valerie and Felicity were all wiping their eyes and nodding wistfully.

Smiling, Lisa picked up the present and unwrapped the layers of crinkled, white tissue paper. Taking in the sight of the gift she took a breath. 'It's ... great, thank you.' Catching her brother's eye, she dared him not to say a word as she held aloft the slightly wonky teal-green cardigan Winnie had so lovingly knitted.

Dom glanced over, his eyes going wide.

'I love it!' Lisa spoke decisively, before he was able to comment, and folded the cardigan, returning it to the tissue paper in her lap.

Florian's presence reminded Lisa that she hadn't shown Nathan the mural in the nursery. Leaving the new round of visitors to have their baby cuddles they went upstairs. Taking in the sight of the waterfall at Sixt-Fer-à-Cheval Florian had painted Nathan smiled.

'Wow! It's amazing.'

Using poetic licence, Florian had surrounded it with cute animals, including a brown and white cow complete with a cowbell, a mountain goat, sheep and a marmot. Nathan looked more closely before turning his head as he studied the finer details.

'That's funny. I never imagined ducks nesting near a waterfall.'

'It's an eagle.' Lisa giggled.

Nathan looked back at the mural. 'Oh, God. You let your mum help didn't you?'

Lisa laughed. 'Shhh, she'll hear you.'

Nathan quacked before laughing and pulling Lisa in closer for a hug. 'It's perfect.'

Two chaotic hours later, the new grandparents and more than a bit besotted new uncle had gone home. Lisa had hugged Winnie, said goodbye to Florian and thanked Dom many times for his amazing help – as well as making him promise that all foof memories were indeed erased. Lisa hugged Felicity – she was the last of her visitors to leave. Overwhelmed by the events of the day, and feeling grateful for all her friend had done, Lisa gave her an extra squeeze. 'Thank you so much for today, for everything.'

'I'm just a phone call away, any time, just call, and I'll be here,' Felicity affirmed. 'Unless I'm chasing a rabbit of course!'

Lisa giggled. 'Oh Flick, I didn't even ask about Doc—'

'Don't you dare. I don't want you worrying about any of it. Though you might have to explain to your editor about the misuse of the box of goodies she sent.' Felicity grimaced. 'But honestly, I can be The Purrfect Pet Sitter for a while. I've had the best teacher.'

'Aww, thanks.'

'No I meant Fred, he's brilliant with animals.' Felicity laughed. 'I'm encouraging it; can you imagine me having a doctor and a vet in the family?'

Lisa laughed, thanking Felicity again before she opened the door.

'Ah Miss Lisa, Mr Martin, he tell me you have baby now.'

Lisa and Felicity jumped at the sight of Mr Chung before Lisa offered him a big smile and took in what he had said. 'Of course, he did.' *Who needs Facebook to make announcements when your parents have Harold Martin as a neighbour?* Lisa thought, amused at how quickly word had got around. 'Do you want to see the baby, Mr Chung?'

'No. No. Miss Lisa must rest, but I want to give you this … for baby.' The elderly gentleman placed a small square of material in Lisa's hand.

Lisa looked at him confused.

Felicity looked at it, realisation dawning in her expression. 'It's for a quilt. I saw one at Jiggle and Sing. It's for a hundred good wishes quilt. It's a Chinese tradition,' she offered, looking at Mr Chung for confirmation.

Mr Chung nodded enthusiastically.

Lisa looked at Felicity, still none the wiser.

'You collect a square of material and a wish from each of your friends and family. Then you put them together to make a quilt, giving the baby a hundred good wishes,' Felicity explained.

Lisa welcomed the lovely gesture, thanking Mr Chung for his kindness, as she imagined the completed quilt. Returning to her hometown, less than a year ago, Lisa had felt lost and alone, now she not only had Nathan Baker back in her life to stay, a baby and a new home, she had friends and family around her – enough to make creating a hundred good wishes quilt for her baby seem possible.

Before Mr Chung said his goodbyes, he looked at Lisa. 'You be very happy now, Miss Lisa, boyfriend and baby, make your heart grow big.'

With Mr Chung's kind words still in her mind, Lisa snuggled into the comfort of the sofa, Nathan by her side as he held their baby girl. Both still a little shocked from the speed of her early arrival and the mayhem of having so many visitors, they welcomed being alone at last.

Lisa looked at her daughter's precious features: her

button nose, her full head of dark hair, the dusting of fine hair on her forehead, her pink lips, pale eyelashes and the gentle rise and fall of her chest in her baby-gro. Testing the name they had decided to give her, Lisa spoke, 'Bliss. I think it really suits her. She's beautiful, do you think it's OK for me to say that?' Lisa smiled.

'I think it's OK because it's true.' Nathan held Bliss's hand, stroking her smooth skin with his thumb.

Taking in the sight of her family, Lisa felt happier and more in love than she had ever thought possible – with Nathan, with their baby nestled in his arms, and with her life. She knew how lucky she was.

Nathan took a breath and wiped the corner of his eye. 'This is perfect. The three of—'

'Four with Uno,' Lisa added, pointing to the cat sauntering through the lounge door after waiting to make an appearance until everybody had gone.

Nathan laughed. 'OK, the four of us here now – Uno, me, you and our beautiful Bliss. This is perfect.'

'Our perfect moment,' Lisa affirmed, before lifting the baby to kiss her on her chubby cheeks.

When Nathan slipped a new charm on to her bracelet just days later, Lisa felt a swell of happiness. The heart, encrusted with a small single pink stone and engraved with the word *Bliss*, shone in the early morning light. She thanked him with a kiss and welcomed his arms around her. Her bracelet was made to fill with their memories, it already represented so much that was precious to her, and this was just the beginning.

Thank You

Dear Reader,

Thank you so much for reading my book. If you enjoyed *Maybe Baby* please tell your friends, and take a moment to leave a review on the site where you purchased it. Reviews, no matter what their length, help authors and their work get noticed. They really are hugely appreciated.

And if you would like to discover more about my writing you can find my details at the end of my author profile. I enjoy getting my followers involved, occasionally asking for research help, so why not give me a follow, say hello, and join in? I'd love to hear from you.

Carol

x

About the Author

Carol Thomas lives on the south coast of England with her husband, four children and lively Labrador. She has been a primary school teacher for over twenty years and has a passion for reading, writing and people watching. When she is not in school, chasing after her children, or stopping her dog from eating things he shouldn't, she can be found loitering in cafes drinking too much tea and working on her next book.

Find out more about Carol Thomas here:
www.carol-thomas.co.uk
www.facebook.com/carolthomasauthor
www.twitter.com/carol_thomas2
https://www.instagram.com/carol_thomas2/

More Ruby Fiction

From Carol Thomas

The Purrfect Pet Sitter

Introducing Lisa Blake, the purrfect pet sitter!

When Lisa Blake's life in London falls apart, she returns to her hometown rebranding herself as 'the purrfect petsitter' – which may or may not be false advertising as she has a rather unfortunate habit of (temporarily) losing dogs!

But being back where she grew up, Lisa can't escape her past. There's her estranged best friend Flick who she bumps into in an embarrassing encounter in a local supermarket. And her first love, Nathan Baker, who, considering their history, is sure to be even more surprised by her drunken Facebook friend request than Lisa is.

As she becomes involved in the lives of her old friends Lisa must confront the hurt she has caused, discover the truth about her mysterious leather-clad admirer, and learn how to move forward when the things she wants most are affected by the decisions of her past.

Visit www.rubyfiction.com for details.

Introducing Ruby Fiction

Ruby Fiction is an imprint of Choc Lit Publishing.
We're an independent publisher creating
a delicious selection of fiction.

See our selection here:
www.rubyfiction.com

Ruby Fiction brings you stories that inspire emotions.

We'd love to hear how you enjoyed *Maybe Baby*. Please
visit www.rubyfiction.com and give your feedback or
leave a review where you purchased this novel.

Ruby novels are selected by genuine readers like yourself.
We only publish stories our Tasting Panel want to see in
print. Our reviews and awards speak for themselves.

Could you be a Star Selector and join our Tasting Panel?
Would you like to play a role in choosing which novels
we decide to publish? Do you enjoy reading women's
fiction? Then you could be perfect for our Tasting Panel.

Visit here for more details ...
www.choc-lit.com/join-the-choc-lit-tasting-panel

Keep in touch:
Sign up for our monthly newsletter Spread for all the latest
news and offers: www.spread.choc-lit.com. Follow us on
Twitter: @RubyFiction and Facebook: RubyFiction.

Stories that inspire emotions!